"I'm not usually considered conceited."

Clancy glared at Ronan and continued, "But I don't usually make assignations and then fail to have them kept."

Ronan contemplated her moonlit features slowly and in return, Clancy found herself involuntarily studying him. It was very much a man's face, devastatingly masculine . . . and disturbingly handsome. She was astonished by the shivery feeling of appreciation that unexpectedly rippled through her.

"No, I don't suppose there'd be many who would willingly forgo an evening with you, darling." Ronan's mouth took on a crooked tilt. "But since you feel I'm responsible, I suppose it's up to me to at least ensure your efforts don't go entirely unrewarded," he murmured, bending his head toward her with obvious intent.

Kerry Allyne developed wanderlust after emigrating with her family from England to Australia. A long working holiday enabled her to travel the world before returning to Australia where she met her engineer husband-to-be. After marriage and the birth of two children, the family headed north to Summerland, a popular surfing resort, where they run a small cattle farm and an electrical contracting business. Kerry Allyne's travel experience adds much to the novels she spends her days writing—when, that is, she's not doing company accounts or herding cattle!

Books by Kerry Allyne

HARLEQUIN ROMANCE

2479—MIXED FEELINGS
2515—VALLEY OF LAGOONS
2527—SPRING FEVER
2593—SOMEWHERE TO CALL HOME
2647—TIME TO FORGET
2725—MERRINGANNEE BLUFF
2737—RETURN TO WALLABY CREEK
2761—STRANGER IN TOWN
2809—THE TULLAGINDI RODEO
2869—CARPENTARIA MOON
2929—LOSING BATTLE
2947—BENEATH WIMMERA SKIES
2990—MAN OF THE HIGH PLAINS
3037—DARK MEMORIES

DISASTROUS ENCOUNTER
Kerry Allyne

Harlequin Books

TORONTO • NEW YORK • LONDON
AMSTERDAM • PARIS • SYDNEY • HAMBURG
STOCKHOLM • ATHENS • TOKYO • MILAN

Original hardcover edition published in 1991
by Mills & Boon Limited

ISBN 0-373-03145-9

Harlequin Romance first edition September 1991

DISASTROUS ENCOUNTER

CHAPTER ONE

'WELL, what do you think of the idea?'

The arch of Clancy Munro's brows became more pronounced as she gazed at her best and oldest friend in surprise. 'To go—*grape-picking* with Darrell and Warwick? At Mildura?'

Lisa nodded enthusiastically. 'Well, we're both out of work at the moment—and you can make good money at it . . . as we know from when the two of them returned from their stint down there last summer.' Without stopping for breath, she hurried on persuasively, 'After all, it would be something completely different, and Darrell told me he's already been in touch with the owner of the vineyard where he and Warwick worked before, and since the man was apparently quite satisfied with their work last year he's promised to reserve places for them on his team of pickers for the coming harvest as well.'

Still trying to come to terms with the suggestion—and for far greater reasons than her friend suspected—Clancy shrugged. 'That doesn't mean he would be willing to hire us as well, though,' she proposed wryly.

'But Darrell and Warwick said he probably would on their recommendation,' came the swift return, indicating that Lisa had already discussed the idea with the two young men who formed part of the mixed group with whom the girls socialised. 'I mean, it's not as if we'd be goofing off all the time, or anything like that. We're not unpredictable teenagers any more, we're twenty-one years old, and we could do the work as well as anyone else he might hire.' She paused momentarily, her expression turning diffident. 'Besides, I thought a change of scene might help to—well, to take your mind off your mother and stepfather's deaths,' she concluded in a rush.

Although not by suggesting they go to Mildura, of all places! thought Clancy almost hysterically. But of course Lisa wasn't to know that. Ever since her mother had told Clancy as a small child how she had been so callously deserted by Clancy's father the minute he had discovered she was pregnant, Clancy had always claimed that her father was dead.

In those early years it had been a form of protection against the hurt and humiliation of knowing her father had cared so little for her as to be totally uninterested in her very existence. So how could Lisa know that, far from being dead, Clancy's father was in fact very much alive and an orchardist in the Sunraysia district on the border between the states of New South Wales and Victoria—and which was centred on the very city of Mildura!

Now, just the thought of her contemptible father still being alive, while her more deserving mother and stepfather had been killed in a car accident some two months previously, was enough to have Clancy pressing her lips together and railing against the unfairness of it all.

'Yes—well—I appreciate the thought, but I really wouldn't like to leave the house vacant for that long,' she temporised at length. After so many years, she couldn't tell Lisa that her father wasn't dead after all.

'Oh, but that wouldn't be any problem,' Lisa immediately discounted, her tone becoming eager again. 'My sister and her husband would jump at the chance to rent it for a couple of months while their own house is being finished, and you know they'd look after it.' She gave a delighted laugh. 'In fact, the timing's perfect, actually. The fellers plan to leave real early Sunday morning, so that they're way out of Sydney before any great amount of traffic gets on the road, because it's almost six hundred and fifty miles to Mildura; while Jodie and Patrick are due back from their honeymoon on Monday afternoon.' She laughed again. 'And Mum would certainly love having them only two doors away for a while! You know how she's been dreading the thought of them moving all the way out to Camden.'

Clancy nodded and half smiled distractedly as her friend unwittingly tore her attempted evasion to shreds. 'Yes, but——'

'Oh, come on, Clancy, what's the matter with you?' Lisa cut her short by exclaiming. 'I was sure you'd be as keen to give it a go as I am, and it's not exactly as if we're buried knee-deep in employment prospects round here at the moment. So why all the hesitation...?' She lifted her shoulders in a nonplussed gesture. 'You haven't got any special reason *not* to go, have you?'

'No, of course not!' Clancy denied quickly, and with the denial came a sudden fierce reversal of reluctance too.

What had *she* to concern herself about in going to Mildura? If anyone should be concerned that they might come into contact—however doubtful the possibility—it was her reprehensible father! He was the one with the most to lose, and hide. It would merely serve him right if the truth did become known, and the more she thought about it, the more she felt inclined to at least consider ensuring that it did. When all was said and done, why should she care if his standing in the community was damaged, or his marriage wrecked? And that was, only if he could be believed that he *had* been married when he met her mother. He hadn't ever cared how much either

her mother, or herself, might have suffered over the years because of his own conscienceless actions!

With a defiant toss of her tawny-blonde and curling shoulder-length hair, she continued with protective, but feigned, humour at length, 'All right, all right, you've convinced me. If Darrell and Warwick can persuade this man to hire us, we'll go and pick grapes too. I guess it could be a nice change to work outside for a time, although——' she paused, her generously wide mouth taking on a rueful curve '—you do realise, don't you, that out there in the middle of summer, and without any shade, we're likely to be working in forty-degree-and-over temperatures?'

Lisa nodded expressively. 'A good opportunity to work on our suntans?' she suggested in droll tones. 'It's just as well neither of us burns much.'

'*And* that we've already spent most of the summer at the beach,' added Clancy meaningfully, eyeing their smoothly bronzed skins.

'Mmm, you could be right. Although you never know, maybe they'll give us some of last year's vintage to drink in compensation.'

Clancy laughed, showing shining white teeth. 'Except that, as I heard it, it'll be sultana, currant, and raisin grapes we'll be picking, not wine grapes.'

'Oh, that's right, I forgot.' Lisa smiled sheepishly at her mistake. Then, thoughtfully, 'Although I think some of them do go into some types of wines.'

'More than likely,' Clancy was prepared to concede. 'But not without a winery, and since I don't recall either Darrell or Warwick mentioning one of those when they returned last year, I suspect the property where we're likely to be working is concerned with dried fruit production only.'

'Oh, well, it was a nice thought while it lasted,' Lisa accepted goodhumouredly. 'But in the meantime, I guess I'd better let Darrell know as soon as possible that we'd like to go, so he can get in touch with the owner of the property.' Pushing back from the kitchen table where they had been enjoying a cup of tea, she began rising to her feet. 'Do you mind if I use your phone?'

'Help yourself,' Clancy invited easily, standing herself now. 'I'll make us another pot of tea while you're ringing.'

An hour later, it had all been arranged, and once the two girls had decided just what clothes and other items they should take with them, Lisa left.

With her departure, Clancy absently went about clearing away and washing up their tea things, her thoughts on other matters entirely. Now that she was actually committed to going, she felt relieved in a way. As Lisa had implied, a change of scene would probably do her good, for the house was still full of memories of her mother and stepfather that were hard to overcome.

Not that they had ever been a particularly affectionate family—or even a very close one, if it came to that. Her mother had never forgotten what Clancy's father had done—had never allowed Clancy to forget either—and, as a result, it had come to dominate her life ever afterwards. And perhaps with good reason in view of her having been abandoned so ruthlessly and, literally, left holding the baby!

While as for her stepfather... Well, even if he had been somewhat dispassionate and detached where Clancy was concerned, he had at least been willing to give her his name and provide for her through the years—which was a hell of a lot more than could be said for her own father!—and certainly Ron Munro's devotion to his wife could never have been faulted.

In fact, as she had grown older, Clancy had often felt sorry for him, suspecting as she did that he and her mother had never had any children of their own owing to her mother only having married him because she had been pregnant with another man's child, and not because she harboured any great feeling for him. Illegitimate children, and their mothers, had still carried something of a stigma in those days.

Nevertheless, in spite of everything, they had at least done their best to provide a reasonable home life, and for that Clancy had been extremely grateful. There had been one matter they had excelled at together, however, and that had been in the management of their finances. A skill that had often aroused feelings close to awe in Clancy, for notwithstanding Ron's relatively lowly paid occupation as a bus driver, and her mother's as a shop assistant, she could never remember a time when there had been a shortage of anything. The most outstanding example of their proficiency was the house that was now Clancy's. Over the years they had renovated and added to it until, now, it was an extremely desirable piece of property.

And they should have been alive to enjoy the fruits of their labours for many more years to come, thought Clancy despairingly, tears starting to her eyes. She shook her head, trying to put it out of her mind. Nothing could alter what had happened, and right at the moment she had other, more complex matters to consider. Not the least of which was whether, on reaching Mildura, she should do her utmost to avoid any possible contact with her father, or... whether she should actively search him out and confront him with his perfidy.

She had to admit that the latter option definitely held a certain appeal, and there was no doubting that revenge *was* sweet on occasion—not to mention justified too! It would be poetic justice, you might say, for all the bitterness and heartache he had caused her mother, especially, decided Clancy rancorously.

Yes, Barrett Sutherland might have escaped unscathed from the consequences of his actions to date, but that could all be about to change! came the determined vow.

It had been late the following Sunday when Clancy and the others arrived at their caravan accommodation on the Mildura property where they were to work, and there had been little time, or inclination, for anything much after the long drive except to throw something together for a meal, shower, and climb into their sleeping-berths.

In the morning, however, it was a different story, and as they made their way to the pickers' assembly point, the two girls took in their surroundings interestedly, Darrell and Warwick having seen it all before. Cresting a slight rise, they could see to the boundaries of the vineyard, one of which ran alongside a thick belt of red gums that followed the path of the mighty Murray River—the source of the irrigation water that had turned the area from being 'one of the most barren regions in the world', as an early explorer had described it, into one of the most productive in the whole country.

To the west they could also see more grapevines, fields sown to vegetables and melons, stone fruit orchards; while the adjoining property to the east was planted with row upon orderly row of lushly green citrus and avocado trees.

A few moments later they had joined the other pickers, and for a while there was much talking and laughing as names were exchanged, and those who knew others from years past briefly explained what they had been doing in the meantime.

'You must be the group that arrived quite late last night,' one girl deduced while talking to Clancy and Lisa. 'I've already met everyone else.'

'You've been here for a while, have you?' Lisa surmised.

'Well, only a day or so on this place,' the girl qualified. 'But in the area for a couple of weeks. My girlfriend and I have been picking oranges over on Wattle Grove while we waited for the harvest to start here.'

On hearing the name of the property, Clancy froze. 'Did you say...Wattle Grove?' she just managed to query in a constricted voice.

'Mmm, that's right. Next door.' A nod was sent in the direction of the adjoining citrus orchard. 'You've heard of it, have you?'

'I—I...' Aware that Lisa was already beginning to look at her strangely, Clancy swallowed and forced a more natural tone into her voice. 'I guess I must have...or seen some fruit with their label on some time,' she prevaricated. She couldn't possibly have divulged that that was the name of her father's property. She was still attempting to come to terms with the coincidence of that revelation herself!

'Well, the label wouldn't have said "Wattle Grove", because their fruit's marketed under a trade name,' she was informed with disconcerting knowledge.

'Oh, well, I suppose it must have been for some other reason that the name sounded familiar,' Clancy returned as casually as possible, and was grateful when their collective attention was diverted by the owner of the vineyard choosing that moment to begin explaining where he wanted work to commence first.

Nevertheless, as the morning progressed, Clancy found her gaze more often than not concentrated on the orchard next door. Pickers, they had discovered, usually

worked in pairs—one on each side of a row of vines—
and as a result she had even arranged for herself to be
facing Wattle Grove all the time, while Lisa had her back
to it.

Because they ripened slightly earlier, the currant grapes
were the first to be harvested, although with her attention constantly divided—watching whatever activity
took place next door, attempting to distinguish between
workers and those in charge—it wasn't long before the
amount of buckets Lisa was filling with the heavy
bunches of fruit was outnumbering Clancy's. So much
so, in fact, that the other girl couldn't help commenting
on it.

'Come on, Clancy, you're dragging the chain,' she
chided genially as her own fingers continued to cut and
snip swiftly. 'What's got into you? Ever since that girl
mentioned the place next door, you've hardly seemed to
have had your eyes off it!'

Clancy averted her gaze swiftly and, temporarily at
least, kept her attention on what she was doing. 'Well,
I am facing in that direction,' she excused with a pseudo-
casual half-laugh.

'Yes, but you're supposed to be *looking* at the vines
here, not at what's going on over there,' retorted Lisa
drily. Pausing, she wiped a forearm across her brow and
expelled an eloquent breath. As they had anticipated, it
was hot, dusty, and sticky work relieving the vines of
their abundant produce beneath a sun that blazed down
from a cloudless azure sky. 'Why the sudden interest in
the place, anyway?' She stopped cutting for a moment
in order to peer at her friend between the vine leaves.
'It can't be simply because you think you might have
heard the name before, surely?'

Clancy assiduously kept her head bent as she dropped
another two bunches into the bucket beside her. 'Oh, I

don't know, it—it sort of gives you an interest in the place, and besides, it's interesting watching their pickers at work. Did you know they use unsupported ladders which they just throw against the branches of the trees before climbing up them?'

'Fascinating,' declared Lisa in an expressive drawl. 'Perhaps the knowledge will stand you in good stead by allowing you to apply for work there—if they still have any vacancies—should you happen to be given your marching orders from here for being too slow.'

Clancy bit her lip. She hadn't thought of that, and although she didn't know if it was likely, she supposed it could be a possibility.

'OK, point taken,' she allowed in rueful accents and, partly to allay her friend's curiosity as well, for the rest of the day did her best to give her undivided attention to the work at hand.

However, despite her good intentions, her thought processes refused to be so confined. They continued to stray across the boundary between the two properties, and as they did, a plan began to form. She would go over there tonight! she decided. Not openly, of course, but just to have a look around; to reconnoitre the terrain, so to speak. There was no telling what she might discover.

A quick peep through a window or two could give her a valuable insight as to how her father had lived these last twenty-odd years. Not that he'd had to do it as hard as her mother and stepfather had done, obviously. That much was more than apparent already just by looking at the size and evident prosperity of his orchards! she scorned with a derisive grimace. And it certainly wasn't because she was hoping to catch a glimpse of the man who was her father either! she assured herself decisively. No, her only interest was in possible means of retribution for what he had done to her mother, that was all. Nothing else!

Consequently, shortly after nine that evening, and with Darrell and Warwick away visiting friends, Clancy waited for Lisa to fall asleep and then, knowing the other girl wasn't likely to wake again till morning after the exhausting day they'd just experienced, quietly let herself out of the caravan and quickly made her way across to the wire fence that separated the vineyard from Wattle Grove.

Once through the fence, it was easier to remain concealed in the shadows created by the trees, although she still could have wished for a darker night, because in her undeniably tense state the lighter patches between the rows seemed inordinately bright. None the less, it still took her some considerable time, and walking, before she could even discern the lights of the house in order to locate its whereabouts among all the trees. Then, having done so, she was still forced to walk for what seemed miles before her eyes could put any actual shape to the building.

Behind the house, which was built of red brick and had a wide veranda across the front and running down one side, Clancy was eventually able to make out a number of other buildings. One, further away than the others, long and low and constructed of corrugated iron, she guessed to be a packing shed. But it was the house that claimed her full attention as she drew nearer to its surrounding gardens.

Halting for a moment beside the last of the glossy-leaved citrus trees, she abruptly found herself wondering what on earth she was doing there. She really didn't need the tension that was curling so insidiously through her insides at the thought of what she was doing, and until now she really wouldn't have believed that the desire to spy on someone was part of her nature, but it was as if she couldn't help herself, as if something uncontrollable was driving her on, and with a dismissive shake of her head she moved stealthily behind the tree again in order to seek the most concealing route across the more open gardens.

The next moment, as she began to emerge from the shadows on the other side of the tree, Clancy's heart leapt into her throat and she froze into panicking immobility. Not twenty feet away stood a tall and muscular male figure with his head turned fair and squarely in her direction! Was it coincidence, or did he know she was there? Had he, in fact, seen her? The alarming questions skittered through her brain in a nervous rush.

'Well, are you going to come out from there, or do I have to come in and get you?' The hard-edged enquiry, rich with warning, suddenly and alarmingly answered all her questions.

Clancy's pulse immediately raced, and since she knew she couldn't possibly explain her presence, self-preservation had her whirling and taking to her heels. Perhaps the knowledge of having routed their intruder would be sufficient for him not to pursue the matter—or her!

It was only when she raced between two trees in the next row, and heard their branches rustle vigorously, ominously, once more behind her that she realised any such hope had merely been wishful thinking on her part. And then there was no time for any thinking at all, only for exclaiming in a mixture of shock and apprehension, when steel-like arms abruptly wrapped about her legs in a flying tackle that dropped her to the warm, grass-covered ground with a bone-shaking jolt.

'You—you damned idiot! You nearly killed me!' she promptly half spluttered, half panted furiously, her previous nervousness temporarily overcome by her indignation as she both hit out at, and struggled to extricate herself from, her attacker.

Quelling her efforts with infuriating ease, he pinned her on her back instead, his hands imprisoning her wrists on either side of her head, his muscular legs straddling her body so that escape was impossible.

'Then you shouldn't have run, should you?' he countered with a hint of mockery in his voice that only annoyed her further. 'In the dark, how was I to know you were female?'

'Except that we're not *in* the dark here!' Clancy smouldered, glaring at him. 'Or do you always have trouble distinguishing one sex from the other?' Her brows lifted sarcastically.

'From the back, and dressed as you are...' He shrugged expressively, imperturbably. 'However, had my first clear view of you been from the front——' his shadowed gaze surveyed her extremely shapely jeans and T-shirted figure with a leisurely thoroughness that made both her face and her temper burn '—I can assure you no such misunderstanding would have occurred.'

And that was only if it had in the first place! Which she was inclined to doubt!

'Yes, well, now that you've realised your error,' she began deliberately, squirming futilely to free her hands at least from his grasp, 'would you mind getting off me, you big ox?' It was an order, not a request. 'Just who are you, anyway?'

No sooner had she asked the question than Clancy's breath caught in her throat. Yes, just who *was* he? she wondered with increasing anxiety. Since she supposed him to be about thirty, he evidently wasn't her father, but...could he possibly be—a half-brother of hers, maybe?

'The name's King—Ronan King. I happen to be the manager here, and I'll be only too happy to comply with your—er—wishes . . . once you've answered a few questions yourself, darling. So how about we start with your reason for being here, hmm?' A hard note entered his voice again.

With her mind distracted with the relief of knowing he wasn't a relative of some degree, at least, Clancy swallowed convulsively. 'I—well—I wasn't planning on stealing anything, if that's what you're imagining,' she evaded in blustering tones.

'Then why run when I spoke to you?'

Clancy stirred restlessly. 'You—startled me,' she defended lamely.

Ronan King laughed; a very masculine, deeply vibrant sound that Clancy was shocked to find she liked—despite the inherent disbelief it had contained. She would do better thinking of ways to extricate herself from this predicament rather than illogically succumbing to the attraction of her captor! she berated herself vexedly.

'Because I wasn't who you were expecting?' he went on to hazard in slightly mocking accents, and Clancy's stomach constricted.

'I don't know what you mean,' she hedged. He couldn't possibly have any idea why she was there, could he?

'I mean, you're not the first trespasser we've had on this place, and it's been my experience that when people of your age go creeping around at night, they're either up to no good, or they're planning to meet someone for—shall we say?—social purposes,' he elucidated sardonically.

As far as Clancy was concerned, it was also a heaven-sent excuse, and, expelling the breath she had been holding so apprehensively, she gratefully made blatant use of it.

'Yes—well—I guess it appears I've had a long walk for nothing.' She sighed with pretended resignation. 'The creep must have just been feeding me a line, and now he's found someone else.' Her eyes lifted to his in provocative accusation. 'Or he also saw you and was frightened off.'

Ronan King quirked a dark brow, his regard turning wry. 'You're implying it's my fault you've wasted your time?'

Clancy pouted prettily. 'Well, I wouldn't wish to be considered conceited, of course, but I don't usually make assignations and then fail to have them kept.'

Momentarily, he contemplated her moonlit features slowly, taking in the pure oval of her face set with glossily fringed dark brown eyes and framed by tumbling curls of tawny-blonde hair; the slightly upturned nose and mobile, curving mouth.

And, in return, Clancy found herself involuntarily studying him too. He possessed a strong face, the skin deeply tanned. His hair was short and very dark, providing a striking contrast to his lighter-coloured eyes which sometimes appeared grey and sometimes blue. His mouth was firm and expressive, with just enough fullness in the lower lip to make it extraordinarily sensuous, his jaw lean and decisively moulded. It was very much a man's face, devastatingly masculine and disturbingly handsome, she acknowledged, and was astonished by the shivery feeling of appreciation that unexpectedly rippled through her.

His own scrutiny now complete, Ronan nodded idly. 'No, I don't suppose there would be many who would willingly forgo an evening with you, darling.' His mouth took on a crooked tilt. 'But since you seem to feel I'm responsible, I suppose it's up to me to at least ensure your efforts don't go entirely unrewarded,' he murmured drily, bending his head towards hers with obvious intent.

In vain, Clancy tried to wrench away from him, her lips parting in indignant protest. Why, oh, why hadn't she insisted he release her when she had the chance? She must have taken leave of her senses to have so passively allowed him to continue keeping her captive in such a vulnerable position!

Then his mouth was slanting across hers, stifling any further objections, and dismaying her with the perturbing realisation that she liked the way he kissed.

She had intended to continue struggling, to twist her head away, but as his mouth moved against hers, his tongue playing over the contours of her soft lips, all her good intentions seemed to dissolve beneath the heat of his overwhelmingly persuasive mouth.

Against her will, she felt her lips beginning to soften and part beneath the seductive pressure of his. There was a virile quality about him that excited her, that stimulated all her feminine instincts, and the electrifying sensations he was arousing were all combining to defeat her.

She could feel the hard warmth of his muscular thighs clamped tight against her sides, and was suddenly aware that his hands weren't holding her wrists any more, but were now cupping her head, his fingers moving caressingly against her scalp. It was an opportunity to make a bid for freedom, Clancy realised, but her body seemed disinclined to take it, for disconcertingly her hands merely shifted to cling to his upper arms instead.

With a muffled sound of satisfaction, Ronan subsided upon her, sending shocking waves of pleasure undulating through her at the feel of his long, rugged length pressed so intimately to her pliant form. The touch of his body began to engender a throbbing ache in the lower reaches of her stomach, as did the raw contact of his hips moving sensually against her own.

Confused and confounded by her reactions—for heaven's sake, she had only met the man less than half an hour ago!—Clancy shivered helplessly, her head spinning when his kisses deepened in intensity and his seeking, pleasuring tongue filled her mouth, delving into its warmth to taste and tantalise each sweet recess.

Then he was lifting his head to gaze down into her flushed and bewildered features with eyes that were a muted grey in the moonlight, dark and subtly mesmerising.

'Hell, I never expected this to be the result when I left the house for a last check on the place,' Ronan murmured roughly in a thick and faintly unsteady voice.

And he thought she had? mused Clancy feverishly. But then he probably did, in view of the reason he apparently believed her to be there, came the mortifying realisation.

'You're quite something, you know that?' he continued huskily, smoothing a work-hardened forefinger over her still moist mouth, and Clancy could only move her head dazedly, too shaken by what had occurred—still was occurring!—to even reply.

She was stunned by the force of the emotions he had created so effortlessly within her, and against which she seemed to have no defence. Lord, the only thing she knew about him was his name and position here...and he didn't even know *that* much about her!

But when his mouth took possession of hers once more, and his hands found their way under her T-shirt to the silken skin beneath, all such arguments fled as her senses again flared betrayingly in response.

Now he drew her upper lip between his teeth, caressing its soft contours with his tongue at the same time as his fingers released the catch of her bra, and her breath shredded in her throat when he cupped the taut fullness of her breasts in his hands. She wanted to protest, but the hungry probing of his tongue made it impossible, and all the while his fingers stroked and tormented her already hardened nipples until she was arching against him mindlessly and her whole body felt as if it were on fire.

Never had she experienced such a lack of control over herself. Her mind and body seemed to have acquired wills of their own; their only interest a desire for him to continue stirring her senses to such sweetly intense heights.

'I don't believe this... but hell, I want you!' he muttered rawly as he reluctantly lifted his head. In the silvery light his face was taut, his eyes burning with a naked need that made Clancy tremble, suddenly aware of the state of his own arousal, hard and insistent against her hip. Catching one of her hands in his, he moved to draw her upwards as he half exhorted, half entreated urgently, 'Come back to the house with me.'

The house. Her *father's* house!

The enormity of her inexplicable behaviour abruptly penetrated Clancy's consciousness, constricting her stomach and suffusing her cheeks with embarrassed colour, but at least bringing with them a return of some sort of control.

Without saying a word, she caught him unawares by suddenly pushing him away from her, hard, and managed to scramble hastily to her feet before he had time to recover. She didn't even stop to fasten her bra, but simply ran, as hard and as fast as her slightly unsteady legs could carry her, in the direction of the vineyard.

After Ronan's initial startled exclamation, Clancy heard him call out something indecipherable, but she neither slowed nor even looked back. Instead, panicking at the thought that he might give chase once again, she started weaving among the trees, hoping that if he lost sight of her his interest would wane accordingly.

By the time she reached the caravan she was struggling for breath and drenched in perspiration. She had run all the way, and it was a warm night. In fact, she was sure that the sweet smell of grass and warm earth would forever remind her of Ronan King and the thoroughly mortifying events of that evening.

But at least her assumption had been correct, she was able to note in sagging relief. He hadn't followed her. There was no one about but herself.

It was the only success she'd had all night, reflected Clancy ironically.

CHAPTER TWO

THE following morning, Clancy said nothing at all to Lisa about her encounter with Ronan King. Not only would it have been extremely difficult to explain why she had been on Wattle Grove, but she couldn't even resolve to her own satisfaction the reason for what had ensued.

What on earth had she been thinking of? she castigated herself vexedly. It had been so uncharacteristic of her. And to have allowed it to happen with Ronan King, of all people, she must have gone soft in the head!

Obviously he wasn't a man she could ensure she never met again. He was the manager at Wattle Grove; her father's manager, presumably! And as such, doubtless she would come in contact with him again if she went ahead with her plan to expose her father. Her face burnt at the mere thought. Meeting Ronan King again was the very last thing she wanted.

Lord, what could she say? What believable explanation could she give for having permitted such intimacies...for having responded to them so unreservedly? Worse, what if he had happened to mention the episode to someone else—her father, for instance?

The warmth already in her cheeks became a wave that washed her whole body with the heat of humiliation. How in heaven's name had it all got so out of hand? It had been evident that sardonic amusement had engendered that first kiss; her response no doubt surprising him as much as it had herself. But after that... Well, his reaction most likely had been governed merely by a basic male desire, whereas hers...

She shook her head dismissively. She could only suppose it had been an unconscious outlet for the release of tension heightened by his sudden and unexpected discovery of her on the property. What other explanation could there possibly be? she reasoned bracingly.

Nevertheless, during the day, Clancy found her eyes seeming to stray more often towards Wattle Grove today than they had the day before—if that were possible. It wasn't that she was actively searching for Ronan King's tall figure, she assured herself, but rather so she could take evasive action to ensure there was no likelihood of his seeing her in return if she did happen to catch sight of him.

'You've been quiet today,' remarked Lisa conversationally as the afternoon wore on. 'Something on your mind, or didn't you sleep well last night?'

Clancy affected a nonchalant shrug. Through their long association the two girls were always well attuned to one another's moods. A little too well, on this occasion, for Clancy's liking.

'No, just trying to concentrate on filling these buckets,' she dissembled with a slightly forced smile as the cartman added her most recent efforts to the trailer attached to the tractor which would then take the fruit to the tiered racks where it would be spread for drying in the sun. In actual fact, and perhaps not surprisingly, she hadn't slept well the previous night. She'd had the same discomfiting thoughts on her mind then as she did today. She went on with a rueful grimace, 'As you know, I had the lowest number yesterday, and I don't think the boss was too impressed.'

Lisa's lips twitched. 'No, well, I did warn you that you could be paying too much attention to Wattle Grove.' She paused. 'As you also appear to have been doing today, I might add.' She halted again, frowning. 'Are you sure there's something you're not telling me?'

Clancy swallowed. 'How could there be when I've never been here before?' Then hurriedly, with a camouflaging laugh, 'No, since it's all so new, I've just been doing a little too much stickybeaking, I guess.'

An explanation that, fortunately, Lisa appeared to find satisfactory, and nothing else was said on the matter as they both gave their attention to filling as many containers as possible, since the number determined the amount of their wages.

It was late in the day, when they were all returning to their vans, that Clancy finally saw Ronan, and her nerves immediately tightened apprehensively. He was talking to Madeleine Haigh, the daughter of the vineyard's owner, and they were standing right by the path the pickers used to reach their accommodation.

If she hadn't thought it would draw attention to herself, Clancy would have promptly turned back towards the vines again, but as it was she just had to trust his presence was a coincidence—he was a next-door neighbour, when all was said and done—and hope she could remain safely hidden behind some of the others.

'Far out! Who's the hunk?' Lisa's expressive enquiry, of no one in particular, immediately had Clancy's breath catching in dismay.

When a male caught Lisa's interest, she had no reservations about letting him know it, and Clancy could only pray that Madeleine Haigh's presence would prevent her friend doing anything that might possibly draw Ronan's attention in their direction now.

'Oh, that's Ronan King, the manager of Wattle Grove,' supplied one of the other girls with them who was a regular picker at the vineyard. She laughed drily.

'But don't get your hopes up... he's out of bounds, care of Madeleine.'

Except when it suited him, of course! Like last night, for example! amended Clancy caustically to herself, her cheeks warming involuntarily at the memory of his sensuous mouth possessing hers and his hands caressing her naked skin. He was no better than her father! the contemptuous denouncement ensued. Fidelity obviously meant nothing to either of them; only the self-indulgent desire to take their pleasures whenever and wherever opportunities conveniently presented themselves!

Meanwhile, however, the other girl's advice had clearly done little to decrease Lisa's interest, as evidenced by her jauntily sly surmise, 'Although not to the extent that they're engaged, or anything like that, obviously, since I don't see her wearing a ring of any kind.'

'No—well...' Their companion shrugged, her expression turning wry. 'Be that as it may, it's still not recommended to make a play for him... as others here have learnt before now, to their cost.'

'Meaning?' Clancy couldn't refrain from joining the conversation to probe in short tones.

'Just that it's not unknown for those so unwise as to display an interest in what Madeleine considers to be her property to abruptly find their services no longer deemed necessary.'

'You mean you're likely to get the sack simply for showing an interest in him?' gasped Lisa.

The other girl nodded graphically. 'Madeleine is the apple of her father's eye...so whatever Madeleine wants, Madeleine gets.' Her lips twisted. 'Although it's always another reason that's given for the dismissal, of course.'

At last taking her eyes from the object of her interest, Lisa gave a rueful half-laugh. 'In that case—since I've no desire to suddenly discover myself being shown the

gate—I guess I'll just have to deprive him of my scin-
tillating charms, after all,' she joked, albeit with a decided tinge of regret—but much to Clancy's relief, at
least.

'Mmm, that might be best,' the other girl approved.
Then, in a confiding voice, 'From what I hear, both
Madeleine and her father are only too anxiously awaiting the day she becomes mistress of Wattle Grove
through marriage to Ronan, so of course neither of them
is prepared to allow another female within "cooee" of
him if they can possibly prevent it.'

'I see,' said Lisa, grimacing meaningfully, and totally
unaware of her friend's stiffening figure and frown of
surprise.

'But I thought you said he was only the manager of
Wattle Grove,' Clancy put forward more sharply than
she intended. 'How would——?'

'Because Barrett Sutherland, the owner, thinks of him
as the son he never had,' their informant broke in to
explain, guessing what she had been about to ask. 'And
since neither Mr Sutherland nor his late wife had any
other relatives—at least, not of a close kind—it's been
common knowledge for years that Ronan will inherit the
lot when Barrett Sutherland dies.'

Clancy merely nodded, her thoughts and emotions too
turbulent for her to even reply. So Barrett Sutherland
had been married, even if he didn't have any relatives...at least, not of a close kind! she mimicked acidly,
rancorously, in silence. Well, they would just see about
that! While as for the arrogantly male Ronan
King...doubtless it would take some of the wind out
of his sails, too, to discover his employer wasn't quite
so lacking in kin—of a close kind—as he had evidently
imagined!

Pressing her lips together and, temporarily, totally uncaring whether Ronan saw her or not, Clancy stormed past the couple beside the path. But as it happened, Ronan's attention remained fixed on the girl beside him, and in her present mood Clancy couldn't decide whether she felt relieved or thwarted by the fact that his appearance had apparently been a mere coincidence, after all.

Her first intimation that she might have been wrong in her assumption came half an hour or so later as she was returning to their caravan after a revitalising shower in the small ablutions block provided at the rear of the pickers' accommodation. Ahead of her she could suddenly see Darrell, beer can in hand, lounging in the van doorway, and standing outside just below him...the tall, broad-shouldered form of Wattle Grove's manager.

By then, however, her formerly smouldering emotions had subsided, leaving her now with ambivalent feelings. On the one hand, she still didn't really feel ready to face him, and yet, on the other... Straightening her spine, she quickened her pace. Obviously she was going to have to face him some time, so why not now? And notwithstanding her lingering embarrassment for the uninhibited way she had behaved the previous evening, in actual fact didn't he have more reason to feel shamefaced over the incident than she did? Not to mention apparently having ingratiated himself so resourcefully with her father, of course! she reminded herself bracingly.

Nevertheless, as she approached the two men, Clancy still couldn't quite control the colour that rose in her cheeks, or the fingers that twined restlessly about the straps of the toilet bag she carried beneath her towel. Just why *was* he there, anyway? she wondered edgily. Especially in view of his association with Madeleine!

'Here she is now,' she heard Darrell advise the other man, who had his back to her. 'I'll leave you to it, then.' With a smile in Clancy's direction, he disappeared inside the van.

Drawing a steadying breath, Clancy halted a few feet away as Ronan turned towards her. 'You wanted to speak to me?' she was impelled into enquiring, with a vexing diffidence, when he didn't immediately say anything.

'On someone else's behalf only,' he qualified in coldly squashing tones, and she was startled by the unexpectedly hard set of his face, the rigid lines of his body. So different from the night before.

Why, he's having difficulty holding his temper in check, she suddenly realised in astonishment. There was no languid grey visible in his eyes at all now, just a steely, glittering blue that sent a shiver of disquiet trickling down her back. The intensity of his gaze, which was framed by the thickest and longest black lashes she had ever seen on a man, filled her with a sense of unease, but with a supreme effort of will she refused to allow it to show.

Just because he had taken exception to her running out on him last night there was no reason for her to permit him to intimidate her today! she told herself supportively. It had no doubt been a new experience for him! But if he didn't like it, then perhaps he should have restricted himself to Madeleine in the first place.

With her indignation fuelled by such thoughts, Clancy's jaw lifted to a higher elevation. 'Oh? On whose behalf might you be here, then?' she deigned to query at length on a deliberately mocking note.

'Your father's!'

Just the words, without the savagely biting contempt with which they were delivered, were sufficient to have all the colour draining from Clancy's face, and her eyes widening in stunned disbelief as a jumbled mass of thoughts promptly chased through her mind.

Barrett Sutherland had admitted to having a daughter! To everyone? Or just his manager? But her mother had claimed he wouldn't even acknowledge the possibility that Clancy was his! And even though he apparently had—if only to one person—why now, at this late stage?

Besides, how had he even known she was here, anyway? Not that Ronan had even asked, but she had purposely refrained from divulging her name last night, so he couldn't possibly have been the source. And certainly no one else in the district had any reason to connect the two of them. The whole thing was simply too confusing to take in.

Furthermore, her companions all believed her father to be dead. What if they had overheard Ronan's harshly voiced announcement? she despaired, glancing anxiously in the direction of the van. How could she possibly explain? Come to that, how could she even explain Ronan's requesting to speak to her, when as far as they were aware she had never even met him before?

Raising a hand to her forehead, Clancy rubbed it distractedly, even as she prudently put a little more distance between them and the caravan.

'And—and why would you be here on—his behalf?' she stammered weakly, all her former protective assurance having disappeared at his shocking disclosure.

Ronan's lips levelled, the look on his face so derogatory that she flushed involuntarily. 'Because, naturally enough—although ill-advisedly, in my opinion—he wants to see you.'

Quite apart from the information he imparted, just the fact that he had given his opinion—his unwanted opinion!—was more than enough to stir Clancy's feelings of resentment into life once more.

'Then why didn't he come himself?' she demanded. 'Or would that have been *too* public for him?' Her voice became laced with sarcasm.

Ronan's eyes flared. 'With your lover——' a sharp nod of his head indicated the van '—or should I say *one* of your lovers?—looking on, it undoubtedly would have been, but——'

'Now you wait just a damn minute!' Clancy burst in on him irately. 'The four of us share this van for the sake of financial economy only, and both Darrell and Warwick are friends, that's all!'

'The same as the man you were intending to meet last night?' He crooked a derisively disbelieving brow.

Clancy bit her lip discomfitedly, remembering the excuse she had given for being on Wattle Grove. 'I—well—I only said that because...' Breaking off protectively, she hurried to turn defence into attack. 'In any case, that's rich, *you* taking a self-righteous stance! I noticed you weren't precisely averse to an amorous interlude yourself last night!'

'And as I recall, neither were you exactly unwilling, darling!' he had no compunction in shooting back corrosively, and with nothing remotely amiable in the endearment.

Although her face was hot with shame, for the sake of her self-respect Clancy couldn't allow him to have the last word on the subject.

'I—I at least came to my senses before it got entirely out of hand, though,' she defended throatily, but without quite meeting his hard gaze.

Inflexible fingers promptly cupped her chin to ensure their eyes did connect. 'Although only when I mentioned the house,' Ronan taunted, and taking her aback somewhat with his perception. A scornful curve caught at his mouth. 'Did it suddenly make you realise you might actually set eyes on your father, after all? Is that what sent you scurrying off like a hare with a pack of hounds in hot pursuit?' He laughed without humour. 'Well, it needn't have. As it happens, Barrett wasn't even there. He was in town last night.' Abruptly, he dropped his hand to her arm, his grip no less inescapable than before, however. 'But he is at home now, and he wants to see you...although lord only knows why!' Without further ado, he began propelling her towards a white station-wagon a short distance away, and which Clancy only then noticed.

'No!' she protested immediately, resentfully, trying to dig her heels into the soft dirt underfoot, but to no avail. 'I've no intention of going anywhere with you, and—and it's against the law if you try and force me!'

'Then you'd better come of your own accord, hadn't you?' he countered imperturbably, continuing to urge her inexorably towards the passenger door.

'But I'm not even dressed for going anywhere!' She tried another tack frantically. They might have been clean, but not only were her shorts and top inappropriate for such a proposed visit, they were also somewhat well-worn.

Pulling open the door of the vehicle, Ronan turned to subject her to a hard-eyed scrutiny that she found distinctly unnerving. 'For his very first meeting with his only child, I doubt Barrett will even notice what you're wearing...much less care!' he returned implacably, his expression derisive, and Clancy's temper flared.

And whose fault was it that they had never met? she'd like to know!

'Well, I do care!' she stormed, furiously trying to prise free of his grasp. After this, she would be more than happy if she never saw her father. 'You've no right to come here like some—some arbitrary overlord, telling me what I'm to do, and when! I'm not going with you, and I——'

'Hey! What's going on, Clancy?' Darrell's voice suddenly interrupted her, and looking across to the van she saw him make his way down the steps to come to a halt with his eyes fixed unwaveringly on Ronan, while from the doorway Lisa watched anxiously. 'If you need any help...' The offer was left open, the intention unambiguous.

Clancy felt the fingers encircling her wrist tighten as Ronan turned to confront the other man directly, and suddenly the air seemed to crackle with tension, the area between the van and the car become confining as the two men subtly squared off.

'No!' It was Clancy who shattered the heavy silence on an appalled note. She half smiled reassuringly at Darrell. 'Thank you, but no, I—I don't need any help.' And when he didn't look particularly convinced, she added, 'Honestly, it's OK. It was just an—an unfortunate misunderstanding, that's all.'

'But Clancy, why does—er—Mr King want you to go with him?' called Lisa in a troubled voice. 'I mean, you've never even met him before.'

From the corner of her eye, Clancy saw one of Ronan's brows peak expressively at that, and fearful of what he might be tempted to reveal, she rushed into nervously forestalling speech.

'Yes—well—it's a long and—and somewhat convoluted story,' she stammered uneasily. 'I—I'll explain it all when I return.' By which time she hoped to have a plausible story to tell, if not a strictly truthful one.

'So you are going with him, then?' It was Darrell again.

Since it was evident Ronan had no intention of backing down—he wasn't the type—Clancy nodded reluctantly.

Without wishing to be the cause of any further trouble, she realised she really had no option, and after signalling for Lisa to relieve her of the towel and toilet bag she still carried—avoiding her friend's questioning glance when she did so—she at last slid resignedly on to the station-wagon's passenger seat.

'So you've never met me before,' commented Ronan on joining her, flicking her a mocking glance as he set the vehicle in motion and began driving away from the van.

Clancy determinedly schooled herself to impassivity. 'I didn't consider it of sufficient importance to warrant mentioning,' she declared deliberately with a dismissive shrug. If he thought the incident had meant any more to her than it had to him, then he could think again.

'Although you will have to mention it now.' Amusement laced his words, and Clancy bridled at the sound.

'Thanks to your high-handed behaviour!' she snapped uncontrollably. Just how was she going to explain to her friends without telling them more than she wanted them to know? With a disgruntled grimace, she eyed him resentfully. 'You might at least have given me time to dry my hair properly.'

Ronan spared a glance for the still damp strands that curled riotously about her face and shoulders. 'You'll do,' he allowed flatly. He flexed a broad shoulder. 'Besides, as I said, I doubt Barrett will even notice.'

Mention of her father had Clancy's tension increasing at the thought of their imminent meeting. 'Then if he's so anxious to see me, why *didn't* he come himself?' she demanded in protectively sarcastic tones. 'Was he afraid I might refuse to see him?'

'In view of the past, would you blame him for considering that a distinct possibility?' he countered in cutting accents, both shocking and riling Clancy by the seeming implication that somehow she was the one at fault.

As a result, she immediately gibed derisively, 'So to save himself any possible embarrassment, he sent his strong-arm lackey to do his dirty work for him and thereby ensure my compliance!'

Ronan's jaw muscles clenched, the knuckles of his hands as they gripped the wheel turning white. 'No, he didn't send me. I offered to come... against my better judgement!' he ground out in tight-lipped anger. 'But I give you fair warning—I won't be taking responsibility for the consequences, if you ever make a charge like that again!'

Clancy swallowed. No, she had to admit that there was something about Ronan King—an air of authority, of self-reliance, a steely inner strength—that suggested he was a leader, not a follower. A man who was not to be manipulated, intimidated, or duped. But at the same time, even allowing for the fact that she supposed she might have gone a little overboard in her denunciation...

'Then perhaps you shouldn't have been so anxious to disregard my wishes and arbitrarily manhandle me into the car,' she still felt entitled to censure.

His eyes shaded sardonically. 'Would you have come if I hadn't?'

Of course she wouldn't—as his expression told her he well knew. Any meeting with her father she had wanted to be on her terms, not arriving out of the blue, and with her so totally unprepared.

'And that's all that mattered to you? That I came?' She stared at him in a mixture of frowning curiosity and grimacing resentment.

Ronan gave a brief shrug. 'I happen to owe your father more than I can ever repay. I also have a great deal of respect for him . . . and he wanted to see his daughter,' he advised simply. 'It was the least I could do to ensure he got what he wanted.'

'Even to the extent of perhaps coming to blows with Darrell, if I *had* said I needed help?' Clancy couldn't resist quizzing.

'If that was what was necessary,' he had no hesitation in acceding in the same matter-of-fact fashion, without taking his eyes from the road they had now turned on to. 'I'd told Barrett I would be bringing you back with me, and that's what I fully intended to do.'

Clancy found it difficult to imagine someone like her father apparently inspiring such loyalty. But then, she recalled, Ronan had a very good reason to be loyal. Wattle Grove. The property he was going to inherit! No doubt he would consider it worth taking a few blows for a reward like that.

And that was, only if he'd had the worst of it, in any case, the sudden thought ensued as she covertly studied her companion from beneath her long, sweeping lashes. He certainly gave the impression of being more than able to take care of himself, in any situation. The night before, in the darkness, she had realised just how broad his shoulders really were, how sharply defined the corded muscles of his deeply tanned arms, exposed now by the moulding, short sleeves of his dark blue knit shirt.

Unconsciously, her gaze continued down to his hands. Wide and strong, with long blunt fingers, they were powerful hands, capable, hardened by years of manual work, and definitely qualified to deal effectively with any challenge Darrell might have mounted. That his hands could also be gentle Clancy knew from personal experience, abruptly remembering how sensitively they had moved over her naked flesh the night before, touching, arousing, until she . . .

Horrified at the direction of her thoughts, she swung her gaze away swiftly to stare out of the window, forcing her mind to concentrate on the immediate. They had almost reached the entrance to Wattle Grove now, and every nerve in her body tightened ungovernably at the thought of the coming meeting. It also brought to the fore one particular question that had been niggling at her ever since Ronan's arrival.

'So just how did——' she paused, unwilling and unable to bring herself to say 'my father' aloud '—he discover I was even in the district?' she queried tensely in a low voice.

Ronan's lips curled. '*He* is your father, Clancy, and the least you can do is have the decency to acknowledge him as such!' he slated, obviously alert to her evasion.

Clancy's heartbeat accelerated with anger. Her, have the decency! After the way Barrett Sutherland had behaved all these years!

'And I'll thank *you* to keep your strictures for those who want them, Ronan King!' she stormed. 'Because if either you or *he*——' deliberately '—is expecting me to fall into his arms trilling, "Dad!" in the best hearts-and-flowers fashion, then you've got a big disappointment coming!'

'And where you're concerned, I doubt that's possible, you disobliging, cold-hearted little ingrate!' His voice sliced at her savagely. 'But if you do or say anything to distress that man, you'll have me to answer to, believe me!'

Ignoring the chill of apprehension that momentarily assailed her, Clancy angled her head defiantly. 'I'm positively quaking at the knees,' she quipped on a mocking note, even as she seethed inside. Cold-hearted ingrate! Just because she wasn't oozing gratitude for the supreme honour done her by Barrett Sutherland actually, finally, condescending to meet her! For the sake of her pride—she was damned if she was going to let either of them think this meeting meant anything to her!—she kept a rigid clamp on her feelings and went on with a taunting smile, 'And you haven't yet explained how my presence here was discovered.'

Turning in through Wattle Grove's wide gateway on to the gravelled road that led to the house, Ronan returned her smile with an equally aggravating look of his own.

'I recognised you,' he informed her sardonically.

Shock had Clancy's smile disappearing immediately, replaced by an expression of stunned disbelief. 'But—but you'd never seen me before last night,' she just managed to get out.

Now it was Ronan's turn to smile, with evident satisfaction at her discomposure. 'Barrett keeps a photograph of you in the study,' he supplied, increasing her bewilderment still further, if that was possible.

A photograph of *her*? How could he have? Then suddenly there was no time to dwell on that particular puzzle as another, more discomfiting thought chased it from her mind.

'You mean... You mean you knew—all along who I—I was last night when we—when we were...' She stammered to a mortified halt, averting her gaze, her face burning a dull red.

For a moment, Ronan looked across at her, his regard inscrutable, and then he muttered something explosive and expelled a heavy breath. 'No, not then...afterwards,' he revealed in roughened tones. 'In the half-light your features were shadowed, and——' his mouth took on an oblique slant '—my mind was on other things at the time.' A statement that did nothing to alleviate Clancy's feelings of embarrassment. 'It wasn't until I returned to the house, and happened to glance at your photo, that I realised the similarities, which, in turn, tied in with your suspicious presence there.' He flexed a muscled shoulder. 'Since you were using your real name, a few pertinent enquiries this morning did the rest.'

Clancy bit at her lip. 'I see,' she acknowledged faintly. Since she had not realised her father was even aware of her name, it had never occurred to her to use a false one. In any case, it would have presented problems explaining to her friends why she wanted to do so.

But now they were leaving the rows of citrus trees behind and approaching the pleasingly mellow Victorian-style house which, in the light of day, she could see was situated on a rise overlooking a broad reach of the river. It was a beautiful outlook, with the water glinting between the stands of majestic red gums that lined the river's edge, although Clancy really wasn't in any state to truly appreciate it.

A tense knot was forming in her stomach, her heart beating so wildly she could only just breathe, and her throat felt constricted and dry. Oh, lord, why hadn't she stayed well clear of Wattle Grove last night, then none of this would be happening? she despaired.

But it was happening, and as Ronan braked to a halt beside the steps that led up to the porch, and a man's figure appeared on the veranda, it was only by summoning her deepest reserves of will-power that she was able to alight with any semblance of unconcern.

Grimly determined to reveal none of her inner turmoil, Clancy ensured her spine remained rigidly erect as, with Ronan's hand in the small of her back, she went forward to meet her father for the first time in her life.

CHAPTER THREE

'CLANCY! Welcome to Wattle Grove. I'm so pleased you're here at last.'

Barrett Sutherland moved towards his daughter with his hands outstretched, and thinking he meant to embrace her Clancy stepped back quickly, colliding with Ronan who had stepped a pace behind her on their reaching the veranda.

Unfortunately, the feel of his warm, muscular length pressed so close to her only added to her nervousness as she became disturbingly aware of the hard strength leashed in his overpoweringly masculine form.

'I've waited a long time for this day,' Barrett Sutherland continued, clasping one of her hands between both of his, and even though she didn't pull away this time, Clancy stiffened.

Liar! she thought bitterly. You don't have to put on an act for me. Or was it for Ronan?

But conscious as she was of the younger man's earlier warning, all she could manage aloud in acknowledgement was a brief and stilted, 'Mr Sutherland.'

'No, please, at least make it Barrett,' he requested earnestly, still keeping hold of her hand.

Almost as if he expected her to disappear if he released her, mused Clancy acidly, and abruptly realised that he was as on edge as she was.

'I do understand that you can't be expected to think of me in a more familial manner as yet, you know,' he confided in reassuring accents, beginning to draw her along with him towards the fanlighted front door. 'But

41

I would like us to at least get to know each other a little better.'

Taken aback slightly by his 'as yet' comment, Clancy remained silent, but as they entered the wide entrance hallway, she took the opportunity to scrutinise her parent more closely.

To begin with, she had been most surprised at his age—close to twenty years older than her mother—since she guessed him to be in his early sixties, and she couldn't help but fleetingly wonder why her mother had never mentioned that fact.

He was also tall, although not as tall as Ronan, who headed him by a good couple of inches, and sparely built. His hair was a light brown, generously streaked with grey. His eyes were the same colour as her own, a deep dark brown, and she found the likeness rather disconcerting. Somehow it went against the grain to think she had something in common with him, whereas in neither feature nor colouring had she resembled her mother in any way.

His face was lean and intelligent, still handsome despite the lines etched on it, although as she continued to study him, she began to suspect that not all of those lines had been caused by the sun and his age. In fact, the more she thought about it, the more convinced she became that he wasn't a particularly well man. Beneath the overlying bronze of his skin—nowhere near as dark and healthy-looking as Ronan's—there seemed to be a pallor, a certain careworn look, as of someone who had taken on too much and was now paying the price for it.

None the less, as he showed Clancy through to a spacious and comfortably furnished sitting-room complete with high decorated ceilings, and dominated by a wide stone fireplace with deeply cushioned, cretonne-covered sofas on either side of it, she determinedly hardened herself against the feeling of sympathy that had unconsciously overtaken her. In view of his less than gallant conduct in the past, he wasn't deserving of her sympathy, she told herself forcefully as she reluctantly took the seat offered on one of the pale blue- and grey-patterned sofas.

Ronan, meanwhile, lowered himself with indolent grace on to its twin opposite her, lounging back against the cushions with his hands locked behind his head, his long legs stretched comfortably before him and crossed at the ankles.

Positioning himself so he could watch her like a hawk, decided Clancy with a mutinous glare, and returned her attention to her father, who hadn't yet seated himself.

'You'd like a drink, I'm sure, especially after picking grapes all day in this heat,' he suggested attentively, obviously trying to please. 'Something cold, perhaps?'

Clancy gave a jerky nod. Certainly her throat had never been drier. 'Thank you. A—a glass of fruit juice would be nice. I'm afraid I didn't get a chance to have a drink before I came,' she said with a meaningful glance at the man opposite, but which merely provoked a look of cool mockery in return. 'Nor to change into more suitable clothes,' she added with another rancorous stare.

Ignorant of the circumstances, yet evidently aware of the undercurrent between the two of them, Barrett looked from one to the other indecisively and then did his best to pass the matter off with a smile.

'Yes—well—you look perfectly fine to me,' he hurried to assure her. Which comment earned Clancy a goading 'I told you so,' look from Ronan. 'And, of course, a fruit juice presents no problem.' He started to turn in the direction of the doorway.

'I'll get it.' Ronan's offer had him halting again as the younger man rose lithely to his feet once more. 'You stay and talk.' His mouth shaped ironically. 'She'll probably prefer your company to mine, anyway.'

Clancy wasn't so sure, and pressed her lips together vexedly, but as he continued on out of the room there appeared little she could do about it.

'I gather you—er—took exception to Ronan bringing you here this afternoon,' Barrett deduced on a disappointed note once the other man was out of earshot, seating himself beside her.

With the perfect opportunity staring her in the face for saying exactly how she felt, Clancy suddenly, inexplicably, found she couldn't do it.

Instead, she dissembled, 'More—to his manner of doing so.'

'I'm sorry,' Barrett said with such an apologetic expression that, once again, she felt a stirring of sympathy within her. 'But you have to understand that he's very protective of me, so when I said I'd like to see you...' He half smiled ruefully. 'I suppose I should have known that would be enough for Ronan to ensure the meeting occurred...no matter what the obstacles.' His face sobered once more, his gaze turning anxious. 'I only hope he wasn't too—ruthless. Was he?'

Clancy made a disparaging gesture. 'Nothing I couldn't handle,' she claimed with a manufactured airiness, refusing to let him see it had meant anything to her. And for good measure, 'I had intended to contact you, in any case.'

Although the circumstances and the conversation she had envisaged had been altogether different, of course. However, she was discovering it was all very well making such decisions from afar, but she really didn't have a vindictive nature, and, now that she was actually face to face with her father, she really wasn't sure she could go ahead and denounce him as she had been tempted to do.

After all, it wouldn't bring her mother back, or undo the past, and now there was Ronan's warning to take into consideration as well—a warning she suspected it could be imprudent to underestimate.

'Ah—yes,' Barrett exclaimed, his face clearing and assuming a pleased expression. 'Ronan told me he met you in the orchard last night.'

Clancy's stomach tightened, and she could feel her colour rising uncontrollably as she wondered just what else had been told him about that disastrous encounter.

'Mmm, I was trying to—to locate the house,' she hedged uneasily.

'But why on earth didn't you tell him who you were?' her father puzzled. 'As it was, it wasn't until he recognised the photograph I have of you in the study that we even realised you were in the area.'

At that moment Ronan returned with her drink, as well as a can of beer each for her father and himself and, on distributing the drinks, made it plain he had overheard Barrett's last question by answering it for her.

'I rather think that, by then, she had other things on her mind,' he proposed in a sardonic drawl.

Remembering when he had made the identical remark concerning himself, Clancy hardly knew where to look as her whole body seemed to become suffused with the heat of embarrassment.

'Why? You didn't threaten her when you discovered her on the property, did you?' put in Barrett worriedly.

Subsiding on to the other sofa again, Ronan shook his head. 'Oh, no, quite the opposite. I did my utmost to make her feel—welcome.' He paused, his eyes filling with chafing amusement. 'As I'm sure Clancy will agree.'

His accompanying glance was taunting, and it was all Clancy could do to stop herself from throwing her glass at him as her fingers clenched tightly about it. The miserable, low-life worm! He wasn't going to amuse himself at her expense just because his ego had been deflated when she'd run out on him the night before. Resolutely curbing the anger that raged through her like a river in spate, she gave an indifferent shrug.

'I hadn't really given it much thought,' she rejoined in nonchalantly dismissive tones. 'Probably because it was only of passing interest to me.' She allowed herself a small, disdainful smile... although she was considerably less satisfied with the manner in which he merely quirked a challenging brow in response.

Conceited oaf! she promptly scorned. Did he think he was utterly irresistible to all women? The fact that she had come perturbingly close to surrendering to him herself less than twenty-four hours ago, she studiously avoided contemplating.

'Yes, well, at least you're here now, and that's what's most important,' inserted Barrett soothingly, apparently sensing the subdued antagonism once more. He eyed Clancy with poignant enthusiasm. 'So what made you come to Mildura after all this time?'

Clancy kept her expression deliberately offhand. It certainly hadn't been specifically to see him, if that was what he was thinking, or hoping. And why should she be the one expected to make the effort, in any case? *He* had done nothing but ignore her over the years!

'My friends persuaded me to come,' she told him carelessly. 'With the possibility of wages somewhere between four hundred and a thousand dollars a week, it was an improvement on the dole.'

Some of the light went out of his eyes, and Clancy steeled herself against the traitorous flicker of remorse that assailed her. 'I see,' he acknowledged quietly. Then, recovering slightly, 'Although Estelle didn't offer any objections to your coming, presumably.'

Sudden pain gnawed at Clancy's chest. 'Mum and my stepfather were killed in a car accident a couple of months ago,' she informed him stonily. As if it would mean anything to him!

'Ron too!' he exclaimed, astounding her that he knew her stepfather's name. Come to that, how had he known whom to ask for this morning when making those enquiries regarding her own whereabouts? abruptly came the equally confounding thought. 'I'm so sorry,' Barrett continued with an unexpected degree of regret in his voice. Or feigned regret, amended Clancy cynically. 'It must have been a terrible shock for you.' He hesitated. 'But if there's any way I can help—anything I can do . . .' His words tailed off implicitly.

Clancy's spine stiffened in rejection. 'No, thank you,' she rejected in cool tones. 'Whatever required doing has already been done, and my friends have been marvellous in providing all the support I could possibly need.'

Her father nodded. Disappointedly, she suspected. 'And you're financially secure, of course?' he still half hazarded, half stated.

Clancy pressed her lips together, thinking it was a pity he hadn't bothered to ask that of her mother when he'd so callously discarded her. Discarded both of them, in fact!

'Yes,' she answered shortly as a result. 'Fortunately, Mum and Ron were excellent money managers.' A touch of uncontrollable sarcasm surfaced.

'Very providential!' Ronan suddenly entered the conversation on an acid note, and Clancy rounded on him immediately.

'And what's that supposed to mean?' she flared, even as she noted absently the renewed look of grimness in his expression, the hard set of his jaw. No doubt he considered she wasn't displaying a sufficiently grateful attitude towards her father! she decided, shooting him a rebellious glance.

For a second his eyes clashed with hers in icy contempt, and then they flicked towards Barrett, whereupon he expelled a long, rasping breath and drained the contents of his can with savage haste.

'Forget it!' he grated, crushing the can with his fingers in an action that was ominous in its ferocity. Pushing to his feet, he eyed Barrett sardonically. 'I think I'll go and see about starting dinner.'

'But I want to know...' Clancy began demandingly as he made to leave the room, only to come to a gulping halt, silenced by the sheer intensity of the steely gaze he angled in her direction.

Anger, all the more dangerous for its coldness, flowed from him in a palpable wave, and without conscious thought Clancy deposited her own still half-filled glass on the low table before the sofa and hurriedly gained her own feet.

'Yes—well—I think it's time I was going too, anyway,' she declared a trifle unsteadily. 'Time's getting on, and——'

'Oh, but you've only just arrived,' her father interrupted to lament, rising too. 'I was hoping you would stay and eat with us.'

Clancy couldn't forestall the nervous glance she cast at Ronan, who had delayed his exit the minute he heard her mention leaving—much to her despair. Share a meal with *him*, remain in the same house even, when he looked as if nothing would give him greater pleasure than to murder her! And that was quite apart from the fact that she hadn't wanted to come in the first place. She shook her head jerkily.

'I—I'm sorry, but my friends will—will be expecting me,' she just managed to push out, already beginning to edge her way towards the door.

'But there would be no difficulty getting a message to them,' Barrett immediately tried to reassure her. 'I could ring the Haighs and have Madeleine walk down to tell them that you won't be returning until later.'

Not even the distinctly tempting prospect of the snobbish Madeleine—she had already made it plain to all the pickers that she considered them some lesser form of life—being sent to deliver a message on her behalf was enough to entice Clancy, however, and she shook her head once more.

'That's—er—very kind of you, but—but I'm afraid they will already have cooked dinner for me,' she claimed with fake regret.

'At this hour!' Ronan's voice sliced at her, harsh and disbelieving.

Clancy circled her lips with her tongue. 'I—well—we go to bed early since we start work at seven in the morning,' she excused, attempting to stand her ground.

'So what time do you suppose we start...midday? And I notice turning in early didn't appear to have held such a high priority for you last night. In case you've forgotten, it was after ten before you left here then!' There was a wealth of derision in his tone.

Clancy bent her head. 'That—that was different.' And turning hastily to Barrett in the hope of thwarting any further such discomposingly astute observations, 'I'm sorry, but I just don't want to—to put anyone to any trouble on my account, that's all.'

'In which case there's no problem, is there?' Ronan promptly inserted before her father could speak. 'A phone call is all that's required.' His demeanour relaxed slightly, his expression assuming a somewhat wry cast, as he turned his attention to the older man. 'So why don't you go and ring Madeleine and get her to pass the message along, while your daughter gives me a hand in the kitchen?' He took the few steps necessary to link his fingers about Clancy's wrist and had whisked her through the doorway with him before she even had time to realise his intention, let alone utter more than a gasp in protest.

Once she had recovered her wits, it was a different matter, though, and all Clancy's outraged feelings of resentment at having been arrogantly forced, twice in the one afternoon, into situations she had neither sought nor desired, erupted simultaneously.

'How dare you? How bloody dare you?' she seethed, her fury so choking that she could only just get the words out as she was dragged along behind him. 'Just what gives you the imagined right to ride roughshod over my wishes? It's *my* decision whether I want to come here, stay here, or whether I want to leave!' She drew a panting breath. 'And the minute you take your hand off me, that's precisely what I will be doing—leaving... and you can go to hell!' She pummelled furiously at his arm with her free hand in an effort to force him into releasing her.

Instead, as they entered the large, well-appointed kitchen, Ronan propelled her back against the wall, his eyes as menacing as his continuing grip on her wrist as he bent his head towards her.

'Then you can be sure I'll be taking you with me, you heartless little bitch!' he ground out with jaw-clenched savagery. 'You know damn well your father's greatest wish is to strike up some sort of relationship with you at last, and all you've done is to selfishly and callously keep him at arm's length ever since you arrived!'

Clancy's jaw lifted, her eyes snapping defiance. 'And more's the pity I can't do the same where you're concerned as well!' she retorted, pointedly eyeing his proximity.

'Although last night you had no such complaint—or inhibitions either—as I recall!' he fired back derisively without compunction.

'You bastard!' Her slender hand suddenly cracked across his tanned cheek with every ounce of strength she could muster. Wasn't he ever going to let her forget that fleeting aberration of behaviour?

Momentarily, neither of them moved, the only sound in the room the rasp of ragged breathing. Stunned by her instinctive action, Clancy watched in appalled misgiving the reddening imprint of her hand on his skin. Then Ronan snarled something explicit between his gritted teeth, and powerful arms hauled her hard up against him with rough strength.

Deducing the form of retaliation he meant to take, Clancy began struggling frantically. 'No, Ronan! You've no right——'

'You've just given me the right to do pretty much as I damn well please!' he interposed on a grating note, his eyes glittering within their ebony frames, and crushed her lips beneath his own so fiercely that the breath fled from her body for a second.

With her one free hand trapped against his chest, Clancy tried to push away from him, but he simply captured it and pinned it behind her back along with her other, so that she was held fast within the iron-hard circle of his arms.

The pressure of his mouth was harsh, insistent, and clearly designed to punish, but for all that Clancy found a horrifying, startling warmth begin to spread through her in response. The stimulating feeling of his rugged form moulded so closely to her own was arousing sensations she shouldn't have been experiencing, and which her mind fought hard to deny.

He was merely kissing her in anger, in reprisal, she tried desperately to impress on herself. She should have been disgusted by such a blatant attempt to exert male dominance, infuriated by his arrogant attitude, not submitting to him passively as if she didn't have a will of her own! After all, she hardly knew him really, not to mention the fact that, in view of his unwarranted treatment of her today, she wasn't too sure she even liked him either.

But unaccountably, when his mouth suddenly gentled, to seek and persuade instead of take, nothing else seemed to matter. Waywardly, her quivering lips parted, and the next instant she felt the probing sweep of his tongue as it swirled savouringly, sensuously, about her own.

Unprepared for the maelstrom of emotions that engulfed her, Clancy melted weakly against him, her heart pounding as stormy waves of fire surged hotly through her trembling body. Just as perturbingly as the previous evening, he was enkindling an ungovernable desire, a need, in her that was stunning in its intensity, devastatingly so, she recognised dazedly, and she made a ragged, inarticulate sound in her throat—of desire, helplessness?—as his hands slid down her body to clamp her tightly against his rigidly muscled thighs.

Colour darkened her cheeks as she felt his arousal, a rush of heat abruptly making her minimal clothing feel thick and heavy—and confining. In that instant, she ached to feel his firm flesh pressed against hers, to experience again the galvanising touch of his hands on her naked body. Against his hard chest her breasts swelled, her nipples hardening, and with her arms free now her hands slid around his back of their own volition, her fingertips digging fiercely into the taut muscles.

Ronan shuddered, his mouth devouring hers with increasing passion, and slid a hand up to cup a lushly full breast. The rhythmic play of his thumb as it brushed back and forth across the nipple had Clancy moaning in pleasure against his hotly sensuous lips, and there was a burning ache of longing that was impossible to ignore concentrating in her lower stomach, and which shocked her with the realisation of the depth of her own fervent emotions.

Oh, lord, he made her feel like no other man had ever made her feel before. He also made her want *him* as she had never wanted any man before! she acknowledged shakily. And yet how could it have happened, and so swiftly too? There had been only blazing anger on both their minds when they had first entered the kitchen after leaving her father.

Her father!

As on the night before, it was the thought of her parent that shocked Clancy back into a state of objectivity, and she dragged her mouth free with a gasp.

'Ronan! Barrett could come...' she breathed anxiously, gazing up at him with eyes that were still as languid and filled with desire as his own.

Rather than releasing her, however, Ronan merely bent his head to touch his lips lingeringly to the corner of her mouth. 'Mmm, I guess it's a distinct possibility,' he allowed in a husky, but uncaring tone against her quivering lips. His mouth found its way down the side of her throat. 'I wish to hell he wasn't here, though.' Leisurely, his mouth now moved back to her own again. 'I'm not sure which of us got their come-uppance, but...it seems I like you just where you are.'

Clancy trembled. So did she, she admitted unsteadily to herself. 'B-but when Barrett's finished on the phone...'

'I know, I know,' he groaned thickly, ruefully. Raising his head, he grazed her cheek with his fingers, his eyes a breathtakingly warm, smoky grey as they held hers. 'But take it a little easier on him, hmm? He's wanted this meeting for years.'

Seemingly mesmerised by the sheer seductiveness of his gaze, Clancy swallowed compulsively. How could she refuse him—anything—when he looked at her in such a fashion?

'I—I'll try,' she suddenly found herself promising throatily, moving her head in a helpless gesture...and it wasn't until later, when he wasn't so close to weaken her defences and confuse her thinking, that the doubts came pouring in, along with all the remembered reasons why she shouldn't make matters easier for her father.

It was her chance recollection of Ronan's claim that Barrett had wanted this meeting for years that started it—and brought about a return of her feelings of indignation, tinged with cynicism.

So if he had wanted this meeting for years, why hadn't *he* done anything to ensure it eventuated, instead of merely waiting on the off chance that she might one day visit Mildura? she scorned.

After all, since he apparently knew her mother had married Ron Munro, it surely wouldn't have been too difficult for him to contact them, *if* he had so desired. He could hardly have expected Clancy to search him out instead, when for most of those years she had only been a child. And particularly not in view of his past actions, which had made it more than painfully obvious he had never wanted anything to do with either of them! Moreover, nor could he excuse himself on the grounds of fearing she might not have been told who her true father was, because certainly her mother had gone to great pains to ensure she was aware of every detail on that score.

No, it was only for Ronan's benefit, to appear more compassionate in his eyes, that he was claiming to have wanted to meet her, she decided bitterly. Having mistakenly admitted to having a daughter—and that undoubtedly due to a momentary carelessness, or male bragging, and most likely while under the influence of alcohol!—he was now simply attempting to make it appear as if he were the wronged party!

While as for Ronan himself... Since she was seated opposite him during dinner, it was fairly easy for Clancy to contemplate him surreptitiously. In truth, it disturbed—not to mention disconcerted—her, the effect he had on her when he kissed her, because she couldn't precisely fathom any reason for it. It was also a complication she could well have forgone!

Oh, he was attractive, of course, her thoughts ran on involuntarily, but she had known other attractive men, and certainly none of them had ever succeeded in arousing such feverish emotions so effortlessly, or to such an extent. When all was said and done, how could she even like him when, to date, he had spent most of their time together ruthlessly castigating her for one thing or another? she reminded herself, trying to whip up some protectively righteous indignation.

Then again, just what was he doing kissing *her*, when he was apparently as good as—if not actually—engaged to Madeleine? she wondered with increasing acrimony. Because he was willing to do anything to ensure his inheritance? Even to the extent to making love to her if it meant he could persuade her to be more amenable towards her father? Or because, as she had earlier denounced, he was purely and simply another in the same womanising mould as Barrett Sutherland?

Inexplicably, and certainly unexpectedly, both considerations were rather more depressing than alienating, although there was little time for her to define why that should have been the case as she suddenly realised, with a start, that her father had been addressing her.

'I—I'm sorry, what did you say?' she stammered, uncomfortably aware of the lazy look of amusement on Ronan's face and desperately attempting to remain unaffected. Ignore him, she adjured herself resolutely.

Meanwhile, Barrett waved aside her apology with a smile. 'I was just wondering how long you intended staying in the area,' he explained. 'Just for the grape-picking season, or... perhaps longer?' A hint of hopefulness became apparent in his voice.

Clancy bent her head. 'Umm—no, only for the picking season,' she disabused him on a vexingly contrite note. What had she to feel remorseful about?

'Although, since you mentioned being on the dole, you could stay longer—if you wanted to?' he hazarded carefully.

Clancy moistened her lips, anxious over the direction his thoughts might have been taking. 'I—well—not really, because my friends and I all came together, and—and I wouldn't have any transport home again once they left.' A fortuitous thought occurred. 'Besides, I wouldn't like to leave the house vacant too long.'

'So what would a few more weeks, say, matter?' inserted Ronan casually.

Clancy pressed her lips together. 'Because at the moment it's rented to Lisa's—my girlfriend who's with me here—sister and her husband while their own place is being completed,' she was pleased to be able to advise. 'But once they leave...' She spread her hands eloquently.

Ronan hunched an unperturbed shoulder. 'Then why not just allow—Lisa—the use of it when she returns?' he proposed idly, but no less unrelentingly for all that. 'That way, it wouldn't be left vacant at all.'

And Lisa would be only too happy to help out, of course! Damn, why couldn't he simply mind his own business?

'Yes—well—not that that would help provide me with alternative accommodation in Mildura once the season's finished, however,' she was flustered into retorting in a slightly mocking vein.

'Oh, but you'd stay here at Wattle Grove with us, of course,' Barrett promptly exclaimed enthusiastically.

Clancy stared at him aghast. 'But I couldn't possibly!' she rejected out of hand immediately. Not that she had ever cared much how her actions might be construed publicly before, as long as her own conscience was clear, but... 'I mean, there—there's only one thing people would think if I just moved in with the two of you!' She had already discovered there were no staff of any kind, not even a housekeeper, employed in the house.

'Although what people might think doesn't appear to have worried you unduly when it came to sharing a van at the vineyard with two males,' Ronan was swift to point out in ironic tones, and much to her vexation.

'Is that true?' Barrett stared at her in a mixture of surprise and slightly disappointed disapproval.

Clancy gritted her teeth, resentful at being cross-examined—and by her father, of all people!—and even more furious that Ronan should have placed her in a position where it was considered necessary. Deliberately too, unless she was very much mistaken!

'Yes,' she replied defiantly, baldly, as a result. Then, on seeing the shocked look that came over her father's face, she felt strangely compelled to elucidate a little less belligerently, 'Although we're all only sharing, not co-habiting...as I told Ronan earlier!' She spared that man an expressive stare. 'It's merely convenient and economically beneficial, that's all.' Her chin lifted fractionally. 'If I was going to make love to someone, I certainly wouldn't want an audience around, I can assure you!'

For a time Barrett Sutherland looked as if he didn't know quite what interpretation to put on that statement, and then he dismissed it in favour of suggesting persuasively, 'In which case, there shouldn't be any problems associated with your staying here. And especially not once it becomes widely known that you're my daughter.'

Feeling even more confused by his last remark than he had evidently been by her own, Clancy's brows gathered into an unconscious frown. If he hadn't admitted to having a daughter before—at least, publicly—why was he seemingly so prepared to acknowledge her now? Simply because he was being forced into it because of Ronan's having recognised her?

But if that *was* the reason, why try and persuade her to stay longer...and apparently be prepared to publicise their relationship? That was totally unnecessary, surely. Besides, if it was a case of his having no choice, could he possibly be that accomplished an actor that all his expressions of pleasure at seeing her, his assertions of wanting to get to know her better, were mere pretence?

Admittedly, she had thought so at first, but now... Despite her suspicions, she had to concede that he did seem a kindly man, and there had been too many such instances for them to have been feigned, not to mention an undeniable ring of truth to them... As her mother had also believed all those years ago! the shattering reminder exploded into her brain, and her feelings of confusion were rapidly submerged beneath a wave of contempt once more.

'Wouldn't that make it somewhat difficult for *you*?' she enquired on a sweetly mocking note in consequence.

Now it was her father's turn to frown. 'I don't follow you.'

'Well, since it's obviously not well known that you have a daughter, won't people find it a little odd, to say the least, when you suddenly turn up with one who is not only twenty-one years old, but also just happens to be living with you temporarily?'

Barrett shook his head quickly. 'Oh, no, everyone round here has known me long enough to realise I wouldn't say such a thing unless it were true.'

Because he'd successfully managed to hoodwink them too, over the years?

'Then why keep it a secret until now?' It was the first time Clancy had actually asked him anything concerning herself, and she regretted it as soon as the words were out of her mouth. She didn't want him thinking anything he did, or had done, held any interest for her whatsoever.

Barrett expelled a heavy breath. 'Not because I didn't want it known, believe me. At least, not after my wife's death some ten years ago,' he added with a strict honesty that took Clancy aback somewhat. 'But mainly because there didn't seem much point in mentioning it when it began to appear extremely unlikely I would ever have any contact with you.' He lifted his shoulders in a resigned gesture. 'I thought it would be too painful to have people perhaps asking after you, and me unable to tell them anything in reply.'

An almost overwhelming desire to ask why he hadn't tried to contact her, then, assailed Clancy, but she determinedly fought it down. In spite of the traitorous feelings of sympathy she was experiencing once again, she wasn't going to ask any more questions.

'I see,' she merely said non-committally in lieu.

'Then you will come and stay for a while?'

His touchingly hopeful expression somehow made it impossible for her to refuse. 'I—I... All right, I'll come,' she relented in a rush. Before she got cold feet? she speculated. 'Although I—I can't give any guarantee for how long it will be,' she hastened to add protectively.

'As long as we have some time together, that's all I care about.' Barrett was prepared to make the best of it, his pleasure so genuine and his smile so delighted that, to her surprise, Clancy found herself unable to refrain from smiling back at him in the first really natural gesture she had displayed since arriving.

'Nevertheless, that time period could be extended if Clancy moved here straight away,' Ronan suddenly put in smoothly. 'After all, there's nothing to stop her living at Wattle Grove while she's working at the Haighs'.'

'That's perfectly true.' Not unexpectedly, Barrett was swift to nod his agreement. He eyed Clancy entreatingly. 'Would you be prepared to do that?'

'I—well...' Clancy chewed at her lip distractedly. It was all too much, too soon, and moreover, she wasn't at all sure she wanted to spend so much time in—not her father's company, she discovered to her surprise...but Ronan's! 'B-but there's my friends. We agreed to split all our expenses four ways, and if I leave...'

'Don't worry, I'll be only too pleased to ensure they're not out of pocket in any way,' Barrett offered immediately.

Clancy shook her head helplessly. 'But I can't let you do that!'

Catching hold of her hand, he pressed it encouragingly. 'Why not? I'm your father, aren't I?' And with a warm smile, 'Don't you realise, it would be my pleasure?'

Clancy swallowed. 'That's very generous of you, of course, but I——'

'Please!'

All at once Clancy gave up trying to fight it for the insidious luxury of simply being swept along, and finally gave her assent with a weak nod. As her gaze involuntarily came to rest on Ronan's disturbing figure, however, she could only hope she didn't come to regret her decision.

CHAPTER FOUR

AFTER a night during which sleep had proved elusive, Clancy was already rueing vexedly the momentary weakness that had precipitated her acquiescence to her father's request by the next morning. Had she totally taken leave of her senses?

Not only had she apparently forgotten the loyalty she owed her mother, but she had also made it impossible to continue concealing the true facts regarding her father from her friends any longer. And, after having waited anxiously for her return the evening before, Lisa in particular had been all agog following that forced revelation!

In fact, her questions had lasted well into the night, with the result that all four of them were running late in getting out to the vines after a hasty breakfast the following day, although Clancy couldn't help noticing that it was only herself Madeleine censured when that girl imperiously called her over as they passed her on their way.

'You're late! You should have started almost half an hour ago,' Madeleine snapped coldly as soon as Clancy came to a halt before her.

Honesty had Clancy dipping her head briefly in acknowledgement. 'I'm sorry. I'll work later this afternoon to make up the time.'

'Although only if the cartman and my brother, who's driving the tractor, plus the two men spreading the fruit on the racks, feel inclined to put in an extra half-hour to accommodate you, of course,' Madeleine promptly qualified in cutting accents. 'And since they all began work at the correct hour, that could be doubtful.'

The more so with her to persuade them against it? speculated Clancy with rising acrimony. 'Yes—well—in that case——'

Madeleine cut her short. 'In that case, if you can't manage the work—and you've certainly had trouble keeping up with the others to date—perhaps you would do better seeking employment elsewhere!'

Clancy's breath caught in her throat. 'You're firing me?' she questioned on a partly disbelieving, partly indignant note.

Madeleine waved a haughtily dismissive hand. 'No, merely issuing a warning...*this time*!' she advised meaningfully, sibilantly. Her green eyes, in such striking contrast to her almost jet-black hair, abruptly lost their icy look as they flashed with baleful sparks. 'But if you want to continue working here, I suggest you start pulling your weight in future—and stop thinking I'm here merely to run messages for you!' Her expression turned suspicious. 'Just how did you manage to get yourself invited to Wattle Grove, anyway? Through Ronan?'

Clancy veiled her own eyes with her lashes. So that was what this was all about—Madeleine's proprietorial instincts where Ronan was concerned, and the phone call Barrett had made to the Haighs the previous evening. With all that had happened in the meantime, she had forgotten about the latter. But, since her father had apparently not seen fit to disclose their true relationship to the Haighs when he contacted them, Clancy had no intention of being the first to do so and, consequently, she responded in as deprecating a manner as she could affect.

'No, Barrett Sutherland knew my mother many years ago and merely invited me to dinner when he discovered

I was in the district, that's all,' she temporised with an offhand shrug, and went on quickly in order, she hoped, to preclude any further questions on that particular subject. 'Although I can assure you it wasn't my idea that you be requested to pass on a message to my friends.' She hadn't even wanted to remain for dinner, as she recalled.

None the less, in spite of the conciliatory tone—grudgingly, but prudently, made on Clancy's part—Madeleine continued to eye her narrowly.

'And you won't be repeating the visit.' It was more of a statement—a direction almost—than a question, and Clancy's breathing deepened uncontrollably.

She had no doubt that it was Ronan on the other girl's mind again, and that she was tacitly being told to give him a wide berth, but, despite having come to much the same decision herself, it was still an attempted interference in her affairs that Clancy found wholly unacceptable, and certainly not one she felt inclined to respond to in the same placatory fashion as earlier. Where she went was her own affair, and if Madeleine didn't like it, that was just too bad!

'As it so happens, yes, I will be visiting Wattle Grove again,' she therefore derived no small pleasure from relaying dulcetly. 'In fact——' she was unable to refrain from pausing for effect '—I've even accepted an invitation to live there, as from this afternoon, for the remainder of the time I'm in Mildura.'

'With Ronan and Barrett...*on your own*?' Madeleine shrilled, the look of mingled incredulity and fury on her face sufficient to dispel for the first time Clancy's regrets regarding the decision. 'And whose idea was that? *Yours*, I suppose!'

'Goodness, no! It was all their idea,' Clancy was not loath to discount with a laugh. She had found nothing particularly likeable in Madeleine's superior attitude towards all the pickers before today, but now she was coming to positively *dis*like her.

'*Theirs?*' The older girl, by a couple of years, sounded as if she could hardly believe her ears.

'Well, it might have been Barrett's suggestion originally,' Clancy began, strictful truthful. 'But certainly Ronan added his persuasions.' Due only to the fact that she happened to be Barrett's daughter, she carefully forbore to mention. After all, if Madeleine did but know it, she was probably doing her a favour indirectly by giving her cause to perhaps doubt Ronan's fidelity... which, as she could testify only too well, wasn't exactly as steadfast as the dark-haired girl had apparently believed, or could have wished.

But Madeleine obviously had her own thoughts on the matter. 'I don't believe you!' she scorned, struggling to regain her composure. 'Why would Ronan care where you stayed? Someone who's already sharing herself among two other men?' She gave a derisive laugh. 'No, he's got more self-respect than to ever be interested in someone as free with their favours as you. You're simply trying to cause trouble—out of spite—because I chipped you for being late.'

Clancy shrugged, not greatly caring what the other girl believed, and sincerely doubting she would be receptive to any explanation regarding her own relationship with Darrell and Warwick, anyway.

'Then if I'm not to be even later...' she put forward explicitly, beginning to move away.

'Yes, you had better get a move on,' Madeleine was swift to agree, superciliously. 'You've already had the only warning you're going to get. The next time your work's faulted—for any reason—you're out!' She permitted herself a smug smile, which didn't reach her eyes.

'And then we'll see how long Barrett will be willing to have you in his home—as a *permanent* guest—won't we?'

Clancy's lips parted, two suspicions striking her simultaneously. One, that Madeleine meant to have her fired if at all possible; and two, that notwithstanding her claims to the contrary, she apparently wasn't quite so confident of her hold on Ronan as she had implied. Why else would she care how long Clancy stayed at Wattle Grove? However, on that score she wasn't averse to divulging a little more disappointing information—from Madeleine's point of view, at least.

'Since he's already requested that I remain longer than the picking season, I doubt it would make any difference,' she asserted with an ungovernable touch of mockery, and without waiting for an answer she turned and continued on her way towards the vines.

Lisa was already filling her third bucket when Clancy arrived, and she eyed her friend interestedly, quizzing, 'What was all that about?'

Clancy grimaced expressively as she began cutting and snipping the bunches of grapes hurriedly in an effort to make up for lost time.

'A lecture for being late,' she relayed on a sardonic note.

Lisa's brows first lifted, and then lowered into a frown. 'But so were the three of *us*. Why didn't she say something to us too...or was it in the form of a message to be passed on?'

Clancy half laughed wryly. 'No, the passing on of messages was part of her complaint.'

'I don't follow you.' Lisa gazed at her perplexedly across the vines.

'She took exception to being requested to let you know that I wouldn't be back for dinner last night.'

'But it only took her five minutes!'

Clancy's lips twisted. 'Mmm, but I gather she considers even that too much time to afford lowly pickers. The more so those with the hide to be invited to Wattle Grove.'

'She complained about that as well?' Lisa looked taken aback. Then, pausing, she started to grin. 'Oh, because of Ronan King, I suppose.' And, side-tracked by her own comment, her eyes shone with a lively twinkle. 'So what *is* he like, this man Madeleine likes to keep all other females away from? As spunky as he looks?' She made a rueful moue. 'I wish I was the one going to stay at Wattle Grove. I'd give Madeleine reason to worry, believe me!'

'Although only if you're prepared to take the chance on getting the sack, remember?' retorted Clancy drily, and her friend sighed.

'Oh, yes, that's right—I'd forgotten.' Halting, she tilted her head teasingly. 'Although you still haven't told me what he's like and Madeleine or no Madeleine, I'm just dying to know. For him, I reckon it could even be worth getting fired.'

Clancy bent her head, pretending to be having difficulty in removing one particular bunch from the vine, as unbidden memories of herself with Ronan in the kitchen, in the orange grove the night before, flooded into her mind. Damn! Why did her subconscious have to recall those times, and not the occasions when he had acted so arbitrarily, so arrogantly? came the railing thought.

'In view of the way he was prepared to force me into going with him to meet my father, I'm probably not the best person to ask,' she hedged.

'W-e-ll, I suppose he did have your father to think of,' Lisa put forward consideringly with an apologetic look. 'And, to be honest, I'm a little amazed you were so reluctant. If I'd been you, I know I would have jumped at the chance—no matter what had happened in the past. I mean, we all only get *one* father, and...' She halted, her expression turning puzzled. 'Weren't you even just a little bit curious as to what he looked like, at least?'

As much as she hated having to admit as much—even to herself—Clancy knew she couldn't continue the self-deception any longer. She *had* been curious about him, had wanted to know what he looked like, and, she suspected, she had unknowingly felt that way for considerably longer than she was prepared to concede.

'Maybe a little,' was all she would own to her friend, nevertheless. Her feelings towards Barrett Sutherland were still too strongly governed by the past for her to confess to anything more.

'Well, at least you must have found something compatible about him for you to have agreed to stay at Wattle Grove,' reflected Lisa with a wry laugh for Clancy's less than effusive reply. 'However, to return to——'

'Sorry, but I think that will have to wait for a while,' put in Clancy swiftly in relief on noting the tractor turning into their row, and guessing what the other girl had been about to say. For her part, she was no more comfortable discussing Ronan than she was her father. 'I'm behind as it is, and I want to fill at least another bucket before they're collected.'

'Mmm, with Madeleine already breathing down your neck I suppose it's not the day for taking it easy,' Lisa conceded with a nod, increasing her own work-rate, and Clancy was thankful that, by the time their full buckets had been replaced with empty ones, the soaring and searing heat of the morning was such that it discouraged conversation.

In fact, it turned out to be by far the hottest day they had yet experienced—forty-five degrees by lunchtime, so one of the men on the drying racks told them—and by the end of the afternoon Clancy felt just about ready to drop. As did everyone else, she surmised, surveying the other pickers as they all wearily made their way back to their vans.

Hats had been a necessity, but, like the others, every inch of her skin that had been exposed to the sun's scorching rays was now tanned to a new deep, uniform darkness, as well as being liberally coated with dust— except for where the pouring perspiration had washed it away, of course.

All she wanted to do—all she felt capable of doing— was to collapse on to her bunk with something cold to drink, not even the knowledge that she had picked far more grapes than on the two previous days capable of putting a spring into her dragging steps. What she didn't want was to suddenly be reminded that she was supposed to pack her gear and move to Wattle Grove that afternoon, by finding Ronan already waiting for her at the caravan.

That he also happened to look entirely unaffected by the heat, his jeans and sky-blue cotton-knit shirt fresh and clean, his dark hair damply curling as if from a recent shower, only made her feel even more exhausted and wilted by comparison—not to mention a touch resentful. How dared he appear so overwhelmingly vital and vigorous while she felt more dead than alive?

'You're not ready yet, I take it?' Ronan drawled wryly, lips twitching, as he took in her bedraggled appearance, but despite her brief and disgruntled glare Clancy was just too weary to retaliate.

'Nor likely to be this side of tomorrow,' she groaned with feeling, slumping on to the first seat available—one of two canvas chairs beneath the awning at the side of the van—while Lisa, after an interested survey of Ronan and a promise to provide Clancy with a drink, reluctantly continued on inside to join Darrell and Warwick, who had reached the van before them.

'So what makes you think tomorrow will be any better?' Ronan countered, arching an expressive brow.

Clancy grimaced. 'Well, I hope it won't be quite so hot, for a start.'

'Not that I'd take any bets on that, if I were you,' he recommended in dry accents. 'From the look of it, I'd say today's weather could continue for a while yet.'

Clancy gave another despairing groan at the thought, her eyes closing, and Ronan laughed—a rich, warmly husky sound that, to her consternation, made her blood quicken in her veins, her tiredness notwithstanding.

'Never mind. You'll feel better once you've had a shower,' he asserted.

With her eyes still closed, Clancy shook her head, in rejection of both his claim and the effect his laugh had had on her. 'Except that I don't even have the energy to walk *to* the showers,' she moaned, settling her aching body deeper into the chair.

'So what are you suggesting? That I carry you over there...and wash you myself?'

'No!' she gasped, her eyes flying open again at last, and her cheeks burning as her mind treacherously pictured the scene. 'I just wish you'd go away and leave me to suffer in peace.'

'Uh-uh, darling.' Ronan moved his head in veto, his hands resting on lean hips. 'You promised Barrett you'd move to Wattle Grove today, and that's precisely what I intend to ensure you do.'

Even if Clancy had found the spirit to reply, she would have been prevented from doing so by Lisa choosing that moment to emerge with a cold can of drink, which the seated girl accepted gratefully.

The fact that Lisa continued to hover expectantly beside her chair made Clancy realise, wryly, that her friend was angling for an introduction, and, suspecting that Lisa wouldn't be leaving until she received one, she did the honours resignedly.

It wasn't until afterwards, while the other two exchanged pleasantries, that she noticed that Lisa had also found the time to wash her face and tidy her hair while in the caravan... *and* that she was smiling flirtatiously as she chatted to Ronan with a vivacity that gave no evidence of the utter weariness of which she too had been complaining such a short time before.

Taking a long, savouring drink from her can, Clancy smiled ruefully to herself. She should have known her friend wouldn't let an opportunity like this pass her by. Then, to her surprise and dismay, on seeing Ronan smiling so amiably, so damned *engagingly*, in response—as he never had with her!—she abruptly found another emotion entirely beginning to make itself felt. That it might have been the stirrings of jealousy, she absolutely refused to contemplate. No, jealousy wasn't the reason she was experiencing such unexpected feelings of rancour, she assured herself fiercely. She was merely filled with disgust for the way in which Ronan was prepared to flit from female to female, that was all.

'...so perhaps you could tell me whether Clancy's gear's packed, at least?' she abruptly caught the last of what Ronan had been saying, and expelled a heavy breath on hearing her friend's reply.

'Well, no, as a matter of fact it's not,' Lisa informed him on an apologetic note. 'Actually, there hasn't been time.' She hesitated before flashing him a winsome smile. 'Although I'd be glad to do it, if it would help.'

And particularly if it also helped to impress *him*! thought Clancy with a grimace.

Ronan, meanwhile, inclined his head in acknowledgement. 'Thank you. Since Clancy appears—er—incapable, I'd be very grateful if you could.'

'Yes—well—it *was* very hot and tiring today,' Lisa offered excusingly. Then, with another sparkling smile, 'Nevertheless, it will be my pleasure. I won't be long.' Turning on her heel, she hurried back inside again.

'It seems your friend wasn't as affected by the heat as you were,' Ronan now remarked with sardonic overtones to Clancy, as he seated himself in the vacant chair beside hers.

As if he didn't know just why Lisa had recovered so swiftly! she scorned inwardly. Aloud, she merely mocked in return, 'How perceptive of you to have noticed!' and, leaning her head against the back of the chair, closed her eyes once more. Perhaps it was partly due to the strain of the last day or so, but no matter what he thought she did feel unbelievably tired.

So much so, as it happened, that Clancy supposed she must have actually dozed off, because she couldn't even remember whether he had replied to her last comment or not when her eyes flicked open next as she felt herself moving.

For a moment, she was totally disorientated, and instinctively clung to the nearest stable object . . . which proved to be Ronan's neck as, with an arm about her back and the other under her knees, he swung her effortlessly out of her chair.

'Come on—I know what you need,' he murmured in a strangely thick voice, striding away from the van with her, and Clancy was unbearably conscious of the warmth and strength of the hard, muscled form she was held against, and of the disturbing feel of his hands on the bare skin of her legs exposed by her shorts.

All at once, she also recalled his earlier mention of carrying her to the showers and washing her himself, and her breath caught in her throat.

'Wh-where are we going?' she faltered half apprehensively, half confusedly, still not fully awake.

'To Wattle Grove, of course,' he looked down at her to advise, his breath stirring the hair at her temple, and a tremor curled through her at the pleasant sensation. 'Your gear's already loaded into the station-wagon.' Even as he spoke, he bent to lower her on to the passenger seat of the vehicle, and it was only then that she realised Lisa was standing near by too.

'I'll see you in the morning, then. Have a good time,' Lisa said as Ronan closed the door and made his way around to the other side.

'But—but I can't go anywhere looking like this!' Clancy protested, trying to shake free of the drowsiness besetting her. She turned to Ronan as he slid his muscled length on to the seat beside her and set the engine running. 'Why couldn't you just have left it until later?'

'Because if the last fifteen minutes were any guide, you'd be dead to the world later,' he returned, his mouth shaping obliquely, and with a hand raised in salute to Lisa he started the vehicle moving.

Clancy, perforce, had no option but to call out her own farewell to her friend, and a moment later Ronan continued, 'In any case, I told you I knew what you needed.'

'And that is?' Her gaze turned wary.

'You'll see shortly.'

Clancy pressed her lips together, but didn't persist. The late afternoon sun streaming in through the opened window was merely adding to her feelings of torpor, and she laid her head lethargically back against the blue upholstered seat.

Lord, she had never felt quite so fatigued, and the thought that she had it all to do again tomorrow, and the day after that—for the next two months, in fact, for after the currants came the sultanas, followed by the raisins—only seemed to wilt her further. At the end of the harvest she was either going to be the fittest she had ever been in her life—and the leanest, she decided, certain she must have lost pounds just in the perspiration that had poured off her today!—or she was going to end up a hospital case!

She must have been mad to have allowed herself to be talked into it—no matter how well paid the work was! While as for those who eagerly undertook the task year after year... She shuddered, and listlessly turned her head against the seat to glance at Ronan.

'Don't they have machines for grape-picking?' she all but accused rather than questioned, and his lips twitched at her tone.

'They do, although not everyone prefers to use them,' he told her. 'The same as we don't utilise mechanical harvesters at Wattle Grove. They tend to shake the fruit from the tree and drop it to the ground, which can damage it. And since we grow a first-quality eating fruit, we would rather employ pickers in order to eliminate any such possible damage.'

Clancy nodded, and prepared to look away again, but annoyingly her curiosity got the better of her. 'And do you make all those decisions concerning Wattle Grove, or does—Barrett?'

Ronan flexed a deprecating shoulder. 'We both have an input, but the final decision is mine these days.'

Clancy hesitated, not wanting to show any interest, and yet seemingly unable to stop herself. 'Because— Barrett isn't in the best of health?' she hazarded tentatively, recalling her initial impression.

The abrupt change in Ronan's expression startled her—his mouth immediately levelling into a hard, tight line, and the glance he raked her with cooling rapidly.

'No, Barrett's health is fine—at least, physically, that is,' he bit out with thin sarcasm. 'It's his spirit that's been afflicted!' He paused, a cynical curve catching at his mouth. 'But then, with a daughter like you, I guess that was only to be expected, wasn't it?'

Clancy gasped, her eyes widening in shock. 'Except that he already looked dispirited before he even met me!' she defended indignantly, and with more energy than she had shown for some hours.

'Precisely!'

Once again, his implication that she was somehow at fault made Clancy boil, but not really feeling capable of sustaining a protracted argument she refused to dignify his remark with a reply, and merely gave a disdainful toss of her head in lieu. As before, if meeting her had supposedly meant so much to her father, perhaps *he* should have made an effort to bring it about years ago!

For the remainder of their journey—mercifully short, to Clancy's relief—there was a strained silence in the vehicle. But after they had reached the homestead, yet continued on past it, she found it extremely difficult to refrain from enquiring just where they were going.

Presently, however, after following a narrow track between the gums leading down to the river, Ronan brought them to a halt on a low bank overlooking the water that lapped at a sandy beach a few yards away.

'OK—out you get,' he directed brusquely, alighting himself, and Clancy's brows arched.

'In order to do what?' she questioned, without moving an inch, when he strode round the vehicle and opened her door. 'I'm afraid I'm too tired at the moment to appreciate any sightseeing.'

'Then there's nothing lost, because it wasn't sight-seeing I had in mind,' he retorted with a caustic inflexion. 'Now—out!' He motioned explicitly with his head.

Clancy deliberately turned her face towards the windscreen. 'Not until——'

'All right, if that's the way you want it...' Ronan bent and lifted her bodily from the seat in the same fashion as he had deposited her on it only a short time previously.

Momentarily, Clancy was too surprised to even protest, but when he made no move to set her on her feet before starting for the edge of the bank, she immediately began to struggle *and* voice her objections.

'Ronan! Just what do you think you're doing? Put me down!' And when he paid not the slightest heed, she repeated more vehemently, '*Put me down*, I said!'

'Willingly!' he responded at last in a flat voice. 'I told you I knew what you needed. A cool dip might wake you up...in more ways than one!' And he calmly dropped her into the water a couple of feet below them.

Waist-deep, it didn't take Clancy long to surface again, although when she did so all traces of listlessness had vanished, replaced by a seething fury.

'You contemptible reptile! I'll kill you for that, Ronan King!' she vowed wrathfully, sweeping her wet hair from her face cursorily as she waded towards the beach. Reaching the sand, she snatched up a piece of driftwood and hurled it at him as he made his way around to the head of the beach. 'What's more, you can tell Barrett that there's no way I'm going to stay in that house either, with you there!'

Easily avoiding her missile, Ronan shook his head decisively in rejection. 'Oh, no, darling, you're not using me as an excuse to go back on your word. You're staying, whether you like it or not!'

'That's what you think!' she promptly contradicted on a vehement note as she stormed closer and let fly with another small branch. 'I'm going back to the Haighs' right now...and you can explain to my father exactly why!'

Ducking this time—her accuracy was improving—Ronan regarded her enraged and dishevelled figure with his lips beginning to twitch. 'I doubt it will be necessary...since you're going to have to pass me in order to go anywhere,' he put forward in meaningful tones, and with a confidence that grated intolerably. 'Although I note it has at least succeeded in finally making you call Barrett your father.' His expression turned mocking.

The shocked realisation that he was right had Clancy pausing in mid-throw of her next piece of debris and catching at her lower lip with even white teeth, although not for long.

'A slip of the tongue, that's all!' she dismissed tersely, sending the length of smooth timber winging towards him with all the strength she could muster. The closing range enabled her to almost find her target on this occasion, she noted with satisfaction. 'While as for passing you...' Mere feet separated them now, and, retrieving another weapon, Clancy brandished it belligerently as she approached. 'I wouldn't advise you to try and stop me! Just what in hell makes you think you can dictate what I can or can't do, anyway? King is only your name, not your damned status, you know!' Her voice became imbued with a smouldering sarcasm. The fact that he laughed simply increased her sense of outrage to such an extent that instead of retaining the piece of wood as a deterrent, as she had intended, she now launched that at him furiously as well—and caught him a glancing blow on the shoulder before he could evade it.

'Will you stop doing that?' Ronan ordered in a voice that was partly rueful, partly filled with an amusement that matched the beginnings of unconcealed laughter on his face.

But the idea that he found her attempts at retaliation humorous only fuelled Clancy's incensed feelings even further and, bending quickly, she made to arm herself yet again.

'Oh, no, you don't!'

With a lethal swiftness, Ronan caught hold of her around the waist before she could reach it, but Clancy refused to give in so easily. In the grappling struggle that ensued, she twisted and turned and hit out at him so wildly that in the end he simply wrestled her to the ground, and by straddling her squirming body and keeping her hands pinned to the sand ensured that she was powerless to continue fighting.

'I seem to remember this is where we came in,' he immediately drawled on a dry note, eyeing their positions significantly, and in spite of her unabated fury the memory his words evoked refused to be dismissed.

As then, she abruptly became aware of the disturbingly stirring feel of his muscular thighs pressed so closely against her, of the aura of raw masculinity he exuded, the warmth of him that was beginning to engulf her senses. Dismayed and irritated by the effect he was engendering, she glared at him defiantly.

'Damn you, Ronan! Get off me!' she stormed. 'It was bad enough being soaking wet. Now I'm covered in sand as well!'

Making no move to do as she demanded, he merely arched an expressive brow. 'Then maybe you should have considered that before trying to brain me.'

'So what did you expect me to do? Thank you for throwing me in the river?'

His lips quirked. 'Well, it did at least succeed in restoring your energy.'

That he was right was galling. That he dared to find the situation amusing—at her expense!—was intolerable, and Clancy's breasts rose and fell sharply as her resentment soared.

'So would sleep have done!' she retorted acidly between clenched teeth. 'And with considerably less shock to the system!'

Ronan shrugged imperturbably. 'But which wouldn't have occurred in the first place if you didn't have such an aversion to facing the truth.'

'What truth?' she scoffed, eyeing him askance. Without waiting for an answer, she began struggling once more to wrest herself from his grasp, commanding half wrathfully, half exasperatedly, 'Ronan, will you let go of me?'

Nullifying her efforts with a humiliating ease, he regarded her wryly. 'Is my life going to be in danger if I do?'

Clancy pressed her lips together. 'It will be if you don't!' she averred hotly, and sighed in relief when he at last consented to release her and she was able to put a little more distance between herself and his vexingly disruptive form.

Futilely attempting to brush the sand from her wet skin and clothes, she soon gave up in disgust and started back towards the river. Evidently only another dip was going to remove it, and not that she cared to admit as much—to Ronan, anyway—but after such a long, hot, and tiring day, the water had been decidedly refreshing—no matter how briefly she had remained in it.

'So what truth do I have an aversion to facing?' she enquired negligently over her shoulder and in lightly mocking accents as she waded into the shallows.

As he followed her to the water's edge, Ronan's expression changed slightly, the curve of his shapely mouth taking on a less compromising slant, giving him a somewhat formidable air.

'Mainly the fact that Barrett *is* your father, and even if for no other reason than that, you owe him more than your continual efforts to distance yourself from him...and now, even to attempt to cry off altogether from staying at Wattle Grove,' came his censuring return. He shook his head impatiently. 'For pity's sake, you know how much your spending time here means to him! And you agreed to it!' A muscle suddenly corded beneath his sun-darkened cheek and his eyes shaded with derision. 'Or doesn't your word mean anything to you?'

'Yes, it means something to me!' defended Clancy trenchantly, her own gaze baleful. Just who was *he* to keep criticising her, anyway?

'Although only while everything's going your way, huh?'

'Or when circumstances...or a third party—' pointedly '—make it impossible!' she snapped.

'You're back to using me as an excuse again?' His dark brows arched sardonically.

'With legitimate cause, I would have said!' she rejoined with some asperity, his reminder resurrecting all her resentment for his earlier action. And with it abruptly came the glimmer of an idea which had her beginning to move into deeper water. There was more than one way to achieve her aim, after all, she suddenly realised, and since it was obvious she wasn't going to be allowed to make it by land... 'And that being the case,' she continued in a chafing tone, accompanied by an equally taunting smile, 'then I'll swim back to the Haighs'.' Without further ado, she launched herself into an easy crawl stroke.

'Clancy, get yourself out of there! You're not going anywhere except to your father's house!' Ronan's voice, rough with irritation and laced with anger, reached out to her, but she took great satisfaction in ignoring it.

The water *was* refreshing, and she was starting to enjoy the feel of it cooling her heated skin. Of course, if it also annoyed Ronan and left him with some awkward explaining to do to Barrett, then so much the better! He'd had no business throwing her in, in the first place!

None the less, even from where she was she could hear quite plainly Ronan's fluent curse at her lack of compliance, and her lips curved in gratification. A feeling that proved to be all too short-lived when, without warning, bare seconds later she suddenly felt herself grabbed by the back of her sleeveless cotton shirt and rudely hauled to her feet.

'You reneging, irksome shrew! You're going to Barrett's even if I have to drag you all the way there!' Ronan ground out on an explosive note, shaking her, and then as if to substantiate his threat he began dragging her roughly back towards the beach with his fingers still tightly wound within the material of her shirt.

Taken by surprise by his unexpected appearance, Clancy stumbled and slipped along with him unresistingly for a moment. Her only consolation was the fact that he was now as wet as she was. But then her outraged feelings started to assert themselves and, digging her feet in, she began to battle infuriatedly against his hold.

'I hate you! Let go of me, damn you!' she half raged, half panted, as she twisted and fought to wrench free.

'Uh-uh!' He shook his head decisively. 'I've already made that mistake once today. This time I'll only be letting you go once you're in the car!' he returned tersely, and then muttered a savage expletive when, in retaliation for his voice being so aggravatingly steady and confident, she managed to grab a handful of his hair and pulled as hard as she could. 'You little——!' He broke off, dragging away cursorily from her grasp and, as if losing all patience, wrapped his powerful arms around her in a vice-like grip and lifted her off her feet completely, crushing her against him so tightly that she could hardly breathe, let alone struggle. 'For heaven's sake, what is it with you that you're willing to go to any lengths to avoid striking up a relationship with your own father?' he demanded on a harsh note.

Accepting, however grudgingly, that she was no match for his superior strength now, Clancy tossed her head in a gesture of defiance, but didn't answer. How could she, when she suspected more than a little of her reluctance was on account of him—and the alarming effect he had on her? Like now!

His body felt like steel against hers, and instantly she had become aware of the heat and force, the sheer maleness of him, through their wet and clinging clothing. His muscular thighs strained against hers, his broad chest flattening her full breasts; a touch that made the pulse at her throat suddenly beat faster, and sent a curling heat swirling into her stomach as she felt her nipples harden.

Dropping her gaze self-consciously, she promptly began to feel hotter still on seeing the edges of her shirt gaping wide, the top three buttons evidently having given way to the stress inflicted on them at some time during their tussle. Above the soaked and consequently almost transparent material of her low-cut bra, her breasts swelled voluptuously, seeming to court attention, and in an agony of discomfiture her eyes instinctively flew to his to see if he had also noticed.

As she found his heavily lashed gaze following the exact route her own had taken, Clancy's throat tightened, the ensuing faltering of her breathing having nothing to do with the steely grip of Ronan's arms around her.

With him continuing to hold her off the ground, their heads were on almost the same level, his eyes mere inches from hers when their glances locked, and she couldn't seem to tear hers away. Deep in his smoky-blue gaze there was a turbulent, smouldering look, inherently dangerous—and exciting—and involuntarily she moistened her lips with the tip of her tongue.

Ronan inhaled sharply, and then one of his hands was tangling within her hair, immobilising her head. 'Hell, you do this to me every damn time!' he growled in roughened tones, and fastened his mouth over hers in a hard and compelling demand that wrested a response from her even as she tried to resist.

Before Clancy knew it, her lips were parting beneath his, her tongue willingly meeting and duelling erotically with his as the kiss became more hotly consuming. Reason seemed to have deserted her, leaving only a shockingly mindless desire to surrender to the scorching sensations he was arousing. And as he felt her yield, her body melting against his hard contours, Ronan's pinioning arms at last gradually loosened their hold.

Slowly, ever so slowly, while his mouth continued to claim hers, he slid her down the muscular length of his body in a breathtakingly sensuous movement that sent her blood rioting through her veins, and the stirring feel of him was like a brand on every nerve and fibre of her being.

In a daze, Clancy clung to him for support, her breathing becoming laboured when his mouth trailed to her cheek, her ear, and down to the fluttering hollow at the base of her throat. Then suddenly her eyes flew open with a start, a gasp on her lips as his hand cupped her breast, the nipple rising tautly beneath the damp fabric of her bra.

Before she could gather her wits, Ronan's mouth found hers again, his tongue outlining her quivering lips before pressing inside to possess and savour until she was moaning softly and arching against him in a fever of need. Immersed in the sea of pleasure he was so skilfully stimulating, Clancy was barely conscious of his hands having disposed of the barrier of her bra until she felt the warmth of his fingers directly caressing the aching softness of her breasts, and by then it was too late. Her emotions were already spinning helplessly out of control.

When Ronan's mouth followed his fingers, moistly laving and suckling each of her throbbing nipples in turn, she shuddered at the exquisite sensation, her every sense centred on his enrapturing mouth as a burning wave of wanting surged through her traitorous body.

Oh, lord, what was happening to her? Where was her anger now? Why, of all men, did he have the power to make her defences crumble so waywardly? True, he was uncommonly attractive and flagrantly male, but he was also arrogant and infuriatingly high-handed—the type of characteristics that usually left her cold . . . not on fire as she was now!

Moreover, by his last remark, he seemed to have implied a certain vexed disbelief at his reaction to her too. But then, where men like he and her father were concerned, wasn't that always the problem? the insidious thought surfaced. They just couldn't help availing themselves of any opportunity that arose . . . and, recklessly, she was simply encouraging that conscienceless, free-and-easy attitude!

Nevertheless, while her blood was thudding in her veins, and there was an increasingly demanding ache within her for him to continue what he was doing, it was difficult to resist. She didn't even want to! she acknowledged with shaken honesty.

Only when she felt him beginning to edge them towards the beach, and she abruptly registered the obvious arousal of his lithe, hard body as his hips thrust against hers, was she at last able to muster enough will-power to pull back from him, away from his bemusing hold. There was no mistaking his inclination, and she was all too perturbingly conscious of her vulnerability to his persuasion.

'No!' she protested hoarsely on a ragged breath. 'If— if you must have sexual gratification, I would rather you—you obtained it elsewhere.'

Ronan's chest rose and fell sharply, his own breathing heavy and slightly unsteady as his dark brows arched momentarily. Then a muscle began to ripple spasmodically in his cheek, and a sardonic glitter entered his narrowing eyes.

'That's not the signal you were giving out a moment ago.' His tone was mocking, insolent, his strong mouth curving in a manner that made her shiver involuntarily with foreboding.

Clancy struggled to hold his gaze even as embarrassed colour tinged her skin, and she adjusted her clothing with jerky fingers. 'And—and nor were you conveying anything similar only minutes before that!' she countered defensively. 'You were only intent on berating me then...as usual! So if it's acceptable for you to—to change your attitude as and when it suits you, I'm perfectly entitled to do the same. After all, I didn't *ask* you to kiss me...on any of the occasions that you've done so!' With a contrived lift of her head in dismissal, she turned for the shore.

'But then, you weren't exactly averse to responding either,' Ronan had no compunction in reminding her promptly in an acid drawl that had her face reddening anew and her hands clenching at her sides as she wished for some other form of retaliation besides words. But, of course, she had already tried that, unsuccessfully, once that afternoon.

Inhaling deeply, Clancy forced herself to glance at him over her shoulder. 'Although only until you wanted to get serious,' she asserted with a protectively derisive smile. She had to destroy that masculine self-assurance, make him believe she was unaffected by him, somehow—anyhow—if the time she was to spend in her father's house was to be even remotely bearable. It would be just too disastrous if he knew precisely how fragile her defences against him really were. She went on purposely in an amused voice, 'I mean, a little light-hearted love-play can be—quite pleasurable, but casual sex is something else, and you really should learn the difference. Just because a woman responds to a man's kisses, it doesn't necessarily follow that she also wants to go to bed with him.'

Ronan's eyes hardened to chips of blue ice, his upper lip curling into a contemptuous sneer. 'And there's a name—quite a few of them, in fact—for women like that!' he grated harshly. 'Doubtless, in view of your liking for such—games, you've heard them all before!'

Clancy swallowed, and simulated an indifferent shrug, despite the tremor of trepidation that trickled down her spine at the coldly ominous look on his face. It was as hard and unyielding as granite, and briefly she wondered if it wouldn't have been wiser to have chosen another method for keeping him at a distance. As a foe, Ronan would be implacable, she had no doubt, and just the thought of it was sufficient to have her biting her lip apprehensively.

On the other hand, if he thought her a tease—to use the least offensive of those names he had mentioned— perhaps he would simply ignore her altogether in future, thereby making all her present worries groundless, she attempted to bolster her flagging confidence consolingly as she continued on her way up the beach.

After all, he would hardly be in a position to greatly discomfit her with Barrett always around, *and* most of his free time would surely be spent with Madeleine anyway... wouldn't it?

CHAPTER FIVE

THREE days later Clancy was fired.

Not that it was entirely unexpected. Ever since informing Madeleine that she was moving to Wattle Grove, she had watched the other girl's simmering rancour grow until she could contain it no longer. The fact that Clancy's rate of picking had continued to be less than impressive—her mind steadfastly continuing to dwell on other matters—had not exactly helped her cause, of course. Nor had her late arrival on two of those three mornings due to her having impulsively offered, as much to her own surprise as to Barrett's and Ronan's, to cook their breakfasts for them.

Despite both of them having seemed reasonably competent in the kitchen, it had still been patently obvious that they regarded cooking simply as a necessary chore, and Clancy had, in an unguarded moment of weakness, taken over the role—the result being to inadvertently—though most conveniently, as far as Madeleine was concerned—present that girl with just an extra reason for ensuring that Clancy's employment was terminated sooner rather than later.

None the less, in spite of her dismay at the turn of events, and her slight resentment of Madeleine's unconcealed delight in having seen her dismissed, Clancy was still able to find some relieving humour, if only of the ironic variety, in the situation.

From the remarks Madeleine had made, it had been very evident she believed that firing Clancy would also bring about her immediate departure from Wattle Grove as well—not to mention Ronan's vicinity!—whereas in actual fact it would have the opposite effect. By removing Clancy's reason for absenting herself from Wattle Grove during daylight hours, she had unwittingly ensured that they would spend more time together.

The more so, if Barrett had anything to do with it! rued Clancy with a disgruntled grimace as she added detergent to the dishwasher the next morning, and recalled her father's reaction the previous evening on learning of her dismissal. Apart from a brief moment of commiseration, he had given the impression that he really couldn't have been happier. And not, it transpired, because it would enable her to spend more time with him—as she had assumed—but because it would allow her to spend more time with Ronan! An association he seemed inordinately anxious, and pleased, to attempt to foster, for some unknown reason.

Clancy's first intimation of such an inclination had come in the form of her father's enthusiastic proposal that she should spend the following day with Ronan being shown over the property. Just how Ronan viewed the prospect Clancy had had no idea. He had merely returned her startled and somewhat dubious gaze impassively...or indifferently. But, for her part, the suggestion had brought an immediate resistance and a tightening of her stomach muscles that threatened her composure.

She didn't want to be in Ronan's company any more than was absolutely necessary. In fact, since moving to Wattle Grove she had determinedly done her utmost to avoid him altogether whenever possible. It had seemed the most prudent course, because in spite of everything, and like it or not, she simply couldn't deny that she was unaccountably attracted to him. He menaced her peace of mind, and her equilibrium, making a mockery of all her efforts to ignore him, as well as her constant reminders that he was the womanising kind of man she despised.

Scowling at the pang of regret that assailed her at that last thought, Clancy set the dishwasher going and reluctantly headed for the veranda to meet Ronan with her features studiously controlled and a strong clamp on her annoyingly wayward emotions. She might have done her best to avoid him ever since that discomposing episode by the river, but he had merely treated her with a cool detachment, and now she could do no less, she decided resolutely. The idea of him ever realising the perturbing effect he did have on her was just too alarming to consider.

Ronan was leaning negligently against one of the veranda posts when she arrived, his hands thrust into the back pockets of his jeans, his tall and muscular frame seeming to dwarf the proportions of the porch. Unlike her, there was no tension in him. Rather, he exuded a careless self-assurance, coupled with a lazy nonchalance, that made her unconsciously tilt her chin higher, as if in defence of her own far less than relaxed state.

'You decided to come, then,' he drawled, mockery predominant, as he eased away from the post. 'I thought it more than likely you'd prefer to find an excuse for backing out ... in your usual fashion.'

Clancy gritted her teeth and willed herself not to allow him to goad her into losing control. 'Although *only* if I had attached any importance to it,' she returned explicitly with a dulcet smile. 'I admit that, from choice, I would have preferred someone else as my guide for this tour, but ...' She affected an unconcerned shrug before continuing, 'While as for those prior occasions——'

'Yes, what about those other occasions?' Ronan cut in to taunt sardonically. 'I'd be interested to hear just why it is that you're so reluctant to strike up a relationship with your own father. Curiosity, at least, inspires everyone else in the world to search for and try to make contact with close blood relatives who've been lost through adoption, migration, or other such dislocating circumstances. But not you!' Abruptly, his smoky blue eyes narrowed as they caught hers and held. 'Why? Because you're just too self-centred to care, or——'

'Or maybe simply because I just don't have quite the same reason as you do for falling in with his every wish!' Clancy was stung into sniping, pushing past him to begin descending the steps.

No sooner had she reached the ground than a hand on her shoulder spun her back to face him as he followed her. 'Meaning?' Ronan demanded roughly, no trace of his earlier casualness evident now.

Already annoyed with herself for having given voice to the unguarded words, Clancy shook her head. 'I...it's nothing,' she tried to discount with a deprecating shrug. 'Forget I mentioned it.' She made to continue towards the orchard.

But Ronan obviously didn't intend to be put off so easily. Catching her totally by surprise, he suddenly hooked a forefinger in the front of the V-necked top she was wearing and, before she could do more than gasp, had pulled her disconcertingly close.

'Meaning?' he persisted softly on an inflexible note.

Somehow the very quietness of the query was menacing, doing even more to unnerve Clancy than the nearness of his finger to her suddenly heated skin, and she edged the tip of her tongue nervously over her lips.

'I—well—it's apparently common knowledge that Barrett looks upon you as—as the son he never had,' she stammered, failing miserably to inject the firmness she wanted into her voice.

'And...?' he said intently.

Clancy swallowed. 'Well—if you must know, it also appears to be common knowledge that—that you'll inherit Wattle Grove when the time comes!' she relayed in a somewhat challenging rush.

'So you've decided you're being cheated out of what is rightfully yours, is that it?' Ronan's mouth assumed a scornful curve.

Blinking, Clancy could only favour him with a stunned stare for a moment. 'I...no!' she denied fiercely at length. 'I've never considered I had any claim on Wattle Grove, and certainly I've never assumed it could possibly be left to me.' She shrugged. 'Why would I? I had no idea until I arrived in Mildura that I was Barrett's only child.'

For a second or two Ronan seemed to eye her sceptically, but then an imperceptible shake of his head dispelled it. 'In that case, you'll no doubt be surprised, and comforted, to learn that, contrary to common knowledge, *I* won't inherit Wattle Grove. *You* and I will...in equal shares,' he advised in mocking accents.

'M-me?' Astonishment registered in both Clancy's voice and her face. 'B-but why would he leave half to me when I'd never even met him until a few days ago?' Now it was her turn to shake her head, in agitated rejection. 'No, you must have got it wrong. He wouldn't do something like that.' Not the father she had been told about.

'Why wouldn't he?' Ronan's gaze turned askance as he watched her changing expressions.

'Because—because it doesn't make sense! Because he doesn't even know me! Because it's...' She came to a gulping halt before the betraying remainder of 'twenty-one years too late!' could tumble from her lips. 'Because you and I can't even go five minutes without arguing,' she substituted defensively in lieu.

Ronan arched a sardonic brow. 'Except on those occasions when we've proved decidedly more compatible, of course,' he qualified meaningfully, deliberately stroking his finger across the rising swell of her breasts, and Clancy felt the fiery effect of the galvanising contact clear down to her toes.

'And—and I've already told you the reason for that,' she just managed to push out throatily, taking advantage of his momentarily relaxed hold to pull free, even as she despaired of her body's dismaying readiness to respond to his every touch.

'Ah, yes, that's right, you're only interested in a little flirtation. Nothing too serious.' His voice was as smooth as the smile that slowly crossed his mouth. 'Well, maybe it could prove—diverting, at that.'

Clancy's heart gave a lurch, her velvety brown eyes widening. Oh, lord, what had she inadvertently started? Just what was he suggesting? Moreover, in what way— diverting? As a fill-in when he wasn't seeing Madeleine? She shrank from the thought.

'Except that I didn't say I was interested in flirting with *you*, specifically,' she gibed protectively.

'On the other hand, though, neither did you deny our—er—physical rapport,' he returned in a taunting drawl. 'So if it's games you're after...' He flexed a powerful shoulder and, fearing she wasn't quite sure what, Clancy took a couple of quick steps backward, self-conscious colour immediately staining her cheeks at his lazily amused look on seeing her instinctive movement.

'You're the one playing games, Ronan!' she rounded on him hotly, nettled. 'So why don't you just get on with showing me over the property—which is the only reason

I'm here—instead of either cross-examining me, *or* trying to make something out of nothing?' Swivelling on her heel, she set off along the path leading to the nearest section of the orchard.

Within a couple of long-legged strides Ronan was beside her again. 'You call it nothing, learning that half of all this will be yours one day!' It was a caustic statement rather than a question.

Clancy flashed him a fulminating glare, gritting, 'That isn't what I was referring to!' As she suspected he knew very well! 'Besides, I only have your word for it that I will inherit any of Wattle Grove, in any event.'

'You're calling me a liar?'

'No!' She shook her head irritably, angry with herself for having resurrected the matter. 'I just think you're mistaken, that's all. There's no reason for Barrett to leave me anything.'

Ronan's mouth shaped sardonically. 'You won't get any arguments from me about that, but obviously Barrett feels differently.'

'Much to your annoyance, evidently,' Clancy promptly gibed in retaliation for his first comment. What right did he have to presume to judge her?

Ronan laughed derisively. 'Uh-uh! You're the one challenging the arrangement, darling, not me.'

'No, I suppose going from employee to half-owner is quite a step up, isn't it?' she couldn't refrain from jeering recklessly. Then, as the contours of his face altered, becoming hard and forbidding, she hurried on swiftly, 'Regardless, you can have it all, for all I care. I don't want any of it, anyway.'

Ronan swore under his breath. 'No, you wouldn't, you ungrateful little viper!' he grated savagely, and surprising her that he had chosen to voice his objection to her last remark rather than her first when she knew it hadn't sat well with him at all. It had shown, and still did, in the steely glint of his eyes, the tightly clenched jaw, even the tense set of his shoulders. 'You don't give a damn about anything or anyone except yourself, do you? And if it means disappointing your father, then so much the better, eh?' He shook his head in disgust. 'Hell, I don't know why he bothers with you! But one thing I do know——' he suddenly wrapped his fingers within her hair, bringing her to a standstill and keeping her head immobilised as he bent his own closer '—whether you want a share of this property or not, you won't tell Barrett you don't, or so help me, I'll wring your bloody neck!'

The threat in his voice was so real that it sent a shiver of alarm racing along Clancy's spine, but she was too incensed to care. 'Oh, yes?' she defied, her eyes brimming with rage and resentment as they met his unflinchingly. 'Well, there are some things I'd like you to know too, Ronan! For a start, you don't happen to be in charge of me, so you can go to hell with all your orders and threats! Whatever I do is between myself and Barrett only, and nothing to do with you! You're not the owner of Wattle Grove yet, you know. You're still only an employee, and I wish to hell you'd remember that and just mind your own damned business! It's up to me, *and me alone*, to choose whether or not I say anything to Barrett about any such legacy!'

'And no prizes for guessing the choice *you'll* make!' Ronan almost spat the words out in his contempt. 'The same as it's always been! Nothing that's likely to cause Barrett any pleasure!' His lips curled derogatorily and he withdrew his hand from her hair as if he couldn't stand to touch it any longer.

Indignant colour tinted Clancy's cheeks. 'That's not true! I agreed to stay here when he asked me.'

'And were still looking for an excuse to avoid going ahead with it the very afternoon you arrived!'

'So whose fault was that? If you hadn't thrown me into the river——'

'Doubtless you would simply have substituted another convenient excuse!'

'And if it had enabled me to avoid your overbearing presence, doubtless I would have!' Clancy wasn't averse to agreeing, sarcastically.

Ronan inclined his head, more in scorn than acknowledgement. 'Then it will be my pleasure to relieve you of that presence here and now. Maybe I'd better go and prepare Barrett for what's to come, in any case.' He raked her with a disparaging gaze as he turned on his heel.

'Don't you dare!' she gasped promptly, grabbing at his arm to halt him. 'That's my decision, not yours, and—and I haven't made up my mind yet.'

'Want to keep the bad news for another day, huh?'

Clancy's lips compressed into a resentful, rebellious line. Then, realising she was still grasping his arm— abruptly she became aware of his hair-roughened skin beneath her fingers, warm and taut, the steel-corded muscles beneath somehow suggestive of a raw animal power—she dropped her hand swiftly to her side as if it had suddenly been burnt.

'Wh-whatever the reason, I won't have you usurping my rights, Ronan,' she stammered.

'Won't?' He raised a challenging brow, and she averted her gaze discomfitedly.

'All right, I—I don't want you usurping my rights, then,' she amended jerkily.

'And Barrett's—rights?' His lips twisted derisively. 'Or doesn't he have any?'

Did he mean in the same way Barrett had considered—joke!—her mother's rights? Clancy's head lifted. 'He makes his own decisions—and suffers the consequences—like most others,' she responded in cool tones. Pausing, she fixed him with a deliberate gaze. 'The same as I'm entitled to do.'

For a long moment their eyes clashed, defiant brown with stony blue-grey, and then Ronan gave a harsh half-laugh. 'Yeah, that's what I thought,' he all but snarled at her derogatorily, and, turning his back on her, strode away.

And this time Clancy made no attempt to stop him. It was more than obvious their views regarding her father would never coincide. Ronan evidently only knew Barrett Sutherland as a benevolent employer, a decent and admirable man, whereas she . . .

Exhaling heavily, Clancy worried at her lower lip with pearly teeth as she watched Ronan's departing figure. She still didn't know whether he intended mentioning the matter of her supposed inheritance to Barrett or not, yet she surmised from his last comment that he fully believed she meant to tell her father that it was unwanted.

She sighed again. In actual fact, she hadn't yet decided either way. Mainly, she suspected, because she still couldn't really bring herself to believe her father might leave her half of Wattle Grove. It just wasn't the action of the man she knew her father to be.

Not until dinner that evening did Clancy see Ronan again. He hadn't even put in an appearance for lunch, making her wonder if he wasn't the one purposely avoiding her now. If that was the case, she told herself, she was glad—hadn't she wanted to keep him at a distance?—but to her discomfiture the thought somehow seemed to have a hollow ring.

Conversely, now that he was ignoring her, she found herself watching for him, listening for his footsteps, and she could only conclude that it was because she had merely wanted to prevent herself becoming too deeply involved with him, not to alienate him altogether.

One thing that did provide her with some relief, however, was the realisation that apparently he hadn't seen fit to warn Barrett of her assumed decision concerning the property, after all. If he had, she was certain Barrett would have immediately said something about it to her, but as yet there had been no sign that he even had anything of the sort on his mind.

Instead, he appeared in a more relaxed and contented mood than she had seen him display to date, as evidenced by his cheerfulness during their evening meal. He even seemed oblivious to the fact that not once did Ronan or Clancy so much as address a remark to each other, but studiously only conversed with him, albeit somewhat stiltedly on occasion in her case. Always, in the back of her mind, was the memory of the way he had made use of her mother and then callously discarded her at the time of her greatest need.

'So how did you enjoy your tour of the place today? Did you manage to see everything?' enquired Barrett interestedly of Clancy part way through the meal.

Clancy swallowed, her eyes automatically flicking in Ronan's direction, but when it became apparent he didn't mean to contribute anything, she bit her lip and swung her gaze back to her father.

'Oh—er—well, I didn't manage to get to see much at all, actually,' she disclosed falteringly. After Ronan had left, she had gone for a walk among the trees, but, without being able to ask questions of anyone, she hadn't found it an exactly informative exercise. Now, forcing a casual shrug, she could only hope Ronan wouldn't contradict her ensuing excuse. 'Unfortunately, Ronan had to leave to—to attend to something.'

'Oh? Problems?' Barrett sent a brow-raised glance towards his manager.

Clancy's breath caught in her throat, her eyes unwittingly focused apprehensively on Ronan's face as she waited for his reply. A look that was returned with an unnerving appraisal, a muscle cording beneath his tanned cheek, until a despairing chill of premonition began to curl up her spine.

Then, when she was sure he intended to reveal the truth, she almost sagged with relief to hear him advise, if with decidedly caustic double meaning, 'Nothing worth any further consideration or effort. Just a matter of sorting out attitudes.'

'Oh, staff problems,' Barrett assumed with a nod. 'Maybe you'll have better luck showing Clancy around tomorrow instead, then.'

Ronan's response to that suggestion was an immediate and decisive shake of his head. 'Sorry,' he said without the least sign of regret. 'But I promised Isla I'd visit her tomorrow.' He went on in anticipation, 'And the day after we're irrigating, as you know.' There was the briefest of pauses. 'So why don't you escort Clancy around tomorrow? I'm sure she'd prefer your company to mine,' with a sardonic tilt to one corner of his mouth. 'You are her father, after all.'

'Well, I did finish all the work that needed to be done on the accounts today,' Barrett conceded. 'So if you've no objections to the substitution...' He eyed Clancy with a poignant diffidence that had her spontaneously replying with words she had never expected to hear herself say.

'Oh, no, I'd be very pleased to have you as my guide,' she averred. Although undoubtedly only because it would be a less discomfiting experience—in more ways than one—than with Ronan, she assured herself. 'But only as

long as it doesn't inconvenience you at all, of course,'
she added as an afterthought.

That Ronan believed the addition had been meant as
a possible excuse for backing out of the arrangement
was plain from the expression that edged across his face,
but Barrett showed no such suspicions.

'No, it will be my pleasure,' he exclaimed so de-
lightedly that she couldn't doubt it. His enthusiasm even
extended to his food as he returned his attention to his
meal with increasing appetite to compliment, 'This is
very nice. And your having taken over the cooking is
very much appreciated.'

Clancy merely hunched a deprecating shoulder, her
thoughts determinedly returning to dwell on an earlier
comment of Ronan's. So just who was this Isla he was
visiting? she couldn't seem to help puzzling over. *Another*
girlfriend? She gave an inward shrug. Why should she
care, anyway? If that *was* the case, wasn't it more
Madeleine's problem than hers?

And yet, despite all her attempts to rationalise and
dismiss the matter, annoyingly it remained with her for
the rest of the evening.

Nor had sleep dampened her curiosity either, Clancy
discovered shortly after waking the following morning.

Although it wasn't until after breakfast, and she and
Barrett were about to begin their tour, when they saw
Ronan leave, armed with a box of assorted fruit—
mandarins, grapefruit, lemons, avocados and, of course,
oranges—that she was at last able to satisfy that curiosity.

'So who's Isla, that she gets taken supplies of fruit?'
she asked her father as nonchalantly as possible.

'Isla Watkins—Ronan's aunt,' he supplied conversationally as they made their way towards the orchard.
'She and her husband—extremely grudgingly on his part,

from what I hear—took Ronan in when he was about ten or eleven, I think, after his mother, Isla's sister, had been knocked down in the street one night and killed.'

Clancy nodded, but far from satisfying her curiosity the information only seemed to whet it, and she found herself probing further, 'His father couldn't look after him?'

Barrett shook his head. 'Not so much couldn't, as his new wife wouldn't. You see, Ronan's parents had divorced some years before, and his stepmother didn't want any reminders around of that earlier marriage. In fact, she even made certain they left town altogether some months after that.'

Clancy frowned. 'You mean Ronan's father didn't even bother to visit him?' She could have added, 'Like you didn't bother to visit me?' but decided against it. Hadn't she vowed not to let him know that she cared? None the less, she did pause to wonder why Ronan had so little sympathy regarding her attitude towards her father, when it appeared he had reason to feel similarly rejected himself.

'Oh, I gather he would make an effort and return for a short visit on rare occasions over the years,' she suddenly realised Barrett was saying in sombre accents. 'But since he had other children by then, it seems he was more than happy to leave Isla with the responsibility of raising Ronan.'

'I see,' she acknowledged tightly, struggling hard to restrain her flaring emotions. The hypocrite! That he should so obviously be moved to compassion by the circumstances governing his manager's early years, while not caring in the least about his own daughter's, was enough to make her seethe. But she wasn't going to let him know it meant any more to her than it evidently did to him, she determined with furious bitterness. *She wasn't!* With a couple of deep, steadying breaths, she managed to force the rate of her pulse back to a more natural tempo, but couldn't seem to put the brakes on in the same fashion regarding her inquisitiveness about Ronan. Disconcertingly, that appeared as strong as ever. 'And—and how long has he worked here?' she just had to enquire.

Her father pursed his lips in contemplation. 'Oh, I guess it must be for about twelve years now,' he disclosed at length, adding almost immediately with a grateful smile of remembrance, 'And what a tower of strength he proved to be right from the start! So much so, in fact, that I sincerely doubt I could have kept Wattle Grove going without him at times, and especially during the first few years of his employment.' His expression became tinged with a heavy sadness. 'Those were the terrible years just preceding and immediately after the death of my wife, Judith.' He glanced at Clancy heavy-heartedly. 'She suffered very badly from a severe case of multiple sclerosis which left her disabled for all but the first year of our married life, as I suppose Estelle must have told you.'

Astonishment brought Clancy to a standstill. 'Mum?' she questioned in an incredulous voice. 'How would she have known that?'

Barrett promptly looked as taken aback as she had. 'Because she met Judith. After all, your mother worked here on Wattle Grove in the packing shed for a while,' he went on to disclose, stunning Clancy even further and leaving her face devoid of all colour. It had to be true, she realised shakenly. It would be too easy to disprove if it wasn't. And, seeing her obvious shock, Barrett frowned in disbelief. 'I mean, surely you knew Estelle came from Mildura?' he hazarded.

Clancy could only shake her head weakly. 'She never mentioned it. She was very much a private person where—where personal details of that nature were concerned.' Her eyes became shadowed with bewilderment. 'Besides, when her—death was registered, the place of her birth was given as somewhere in northern New South Wales.'

Barrett nodded. 'I believe that's the region her family came from originally,' he confirmed heavily. 'Or at least she and her mother did—Estelle being an only child, and her father's premature death being the reason they left the small town where they lived when Estelle was little more than a baby, in order for her mother to find better work prospects in a larger centre, so that they eventually ended up in Mildura.' He hesitated. 'You did know that Estelle's mother—your grandmother—also died only a year or so after Estelle left here, though?'

Clancy gave an affirming nod, but despite all her good intentions couldn't refrain from blurting with a discernibly bitter edge, 'Mum always said it was as a result of the shame she'd had to endure after everyone found out about her unmarried daughter's pregnancy!'

'Shame? *Shame!*' her father repeated in astounded and unexpectedly angry tones. 'Estelle's mother, along with two others, died in a fire when one of the lodgers in the boarding-house she operated went to sleep one winter's night with an open radiator too near the bedding!'

Clancy's lips parted. 'I—well—maybe she meant, metaphorically speaking, then,' she put forward shakily, her thoughts in a whirl. 'B-because Mum said her mother wanted nothing more to do with her once she found she was pregnant.'

'Or Estelle wanted nothing more to do with *her* because her mother told her she had no one to blame but

herself for not having been true to Ron Munro in the
first place.'

'You mean, my—my stepfather used to live in Mildura
too?' Clancy gasped, putting a hand to her head, and
feeling as if her whole world were suddenly being turned
upside-down. So that was how her father had known
Ron's name.

Barrett didn't bother to confirm it, but merely deduced softly instead, 'You weren't told that either, I
gather.'

Clancy swallowed and shook her head. 'It wasn't until
they—they died that I even realised he didn't come from
Sydney, and even then when I learnt he'd been born in
Renmark, South Australia——' a mere one hundred
miles west of Mildura '—it still didn't occur to me to
suspect . . .' She broke off, biting her lip, and then burst
out uncontrollably, 'But—why? Why did they apparently keep it all a secret?'

Drawing her arm through his, Barrett patted her hand
consolingly. 'As to that, I can only guess,' he murmured
with a sigh, starting them towards the orchard once more.
'Perhaps they simply wanted to make a brand-new start,
and considered that the best way to ensure there were
no reminders of the past.'

Yes, that must have been it, Clancy decided firmly,
recovering some of her composure. Although if that was
the case, the unwelcome thought intruded, then why had
her mother gone out of her way to ensure that Clancy
was made aware of everything else that had happened
in the past?

It was puzzling, she had to concede, but with a dismissive shake of her head she refused to delve into it
further. No doubt there was a perfectly logical explanation for that too!

CHAPTER SIX

'Now, as you probably noticed from the area around Mildura, without irrigation this is, by nature, a desert region—and the reason we get so much sunlight. On average, between two hundred and thirty and two hundred and eighty days of sunlight a year, in fact,' Barrett told Clancy as they resumed their tour after lunch. 'And to make certain the trees receive plenty of that sun, including the base of the trees because branches do grow down to ground-level, they're planted in a north-south direction in rows twenty feet apart, and we cut their crowns to keep them to a height of around twelve feet.'

'But by not allowing them to grow any taller, don't you reduce the amount of fruit you could produce?' put in Clancy.

Her father chuckled. 'Since each tree can still give us up to five thousand pieces of fruit when they first come into production, and we only retain about a fifth of those on the tree anyway, we don't really want any more fruit on them. If all the fruit *was* allowed to reach maturity the tree couldn't even survive the weight of it, let alone provide the necessary nutrients, and the tree would die.' Leading them down between two rows where the pickers were working, he went on, 'Besides, keeping them to that height also makes it easier for picking, since we prefer to have that done by hand.'

Clancy nodded, watching as the pickers went about nimbly clambering up their tree-supported ladders to fill their satchels with the bright and glossy ripened fruit, and then empty them into the waiting bins which would be taken to the packing shed near the house.

'And they all have to be picked at the one time?' She looked about her with a grimace at the thought. The rows of shiny-leaved trees seemed to go on forever.

'Oh, no,' Barrett was quick to disabuse her of that idea with another laugh. 'Although we do have two main picking times—at least for the oranges which constitute almost three quarters of our total production—we actually pick all year round. The ones being harvested at the moment are Valencias, a summer fruit, while the navels we saw this morning ripen during the winter months. However, since we only ever pick those pieces of fruit that have reached their peak of maturity—to ensure our product is consistently of the highest quality—we maintain a small core of pickers throughout the year to harvest the remainder of the fruit as it becomes ready...plus those other varieties such as grapefruit, lemons, avocados, et cetera, which have their own ripening periods.' Moving further along the row—in fact, approaching the boundary with the Haighs' vineyard, Clancy noted—he continued, 'Of course, that may be all about to change, anyway, because the scientists have now come up with a summer navel, and that could revolutionise the whole industry if they prove as good in field tests as the pre-publicity suggests.'

'Because the public prefers the navels?' Clancy hazarded.

'Mmm, traditionally the winter fruits—in mandarins too—are the sweet fruit, while the summer fruits are the juicy ones. Now, if they've succeeded in combining the sweetness of the winter navel with the juiciness of a summer-ripening fruit... Well, we're all eagerly awaiting the results of those tests, as you might imagine.'

Clancy nodded thoughtfully. 'I suppose you have to keep replacing your trees periodically, anyway.'

'Yes, they range in age from one year to about twenty-seven years. Some others keep their trees in production longer than that, but we have an ongoing replanting programme due to our belief that they should be replaced *before* their production begins to decrease.'

For a while they continued in silence, and then, as a thought came to her, Clancy smiled. 'With so many of them—and not only at Wattle Grove, but all the dozens of other orchards in the district as well—it must smell heavenly each time the trees come into flower,' she mused, visualising the sight.

'Especially since they all come into bloom at the same time, no matter when their fruit ripens,' Barrett declared, surprising her a little with the information. He uttered something of a chortle. 'It must be quite an aphrodisiac, too, if the increase in births at the local maternity hospital nine months later is anything to judge by!'

Clancy laughed. 'I bet the bees don't mind it either!'

'As we also enjoy having them too,' her father averred cheerfully. 'In fact, we have a few hundred beehives here during orange-blossom time. Bees not only improve the cross-pollination of the trees by almost fifty per cent, but they also produce a delicious orange-blossom honey.'

They were almost to the boundary now, and Clancy's attention became caught trying to distinguish Lisa from among those working amid the vines on the other side of the wire fence. Then suddenly she seemed to espy her friend at exactly the same time Lisa noticed her, and as she raised a hand in greeting the other girl hurried around the vines and ran across to the fence.

'I can't stop long, we're short-handed at the moment. Madeleine sacked another two yesterday,' Lisa relayed hurriedly, her mouth shaping explicitly. 'But how are you going? It's been quite a while since I've seen you.'

After making a suitable reply Clancy proceeded to introduce her friend to her father, but realising their time was limited Barrett considerately didn't prolong the pleasantries, allowing Lisa to return her gaze to Clancy.

'Why don't you come and have dinner with us tonight?' she urged. Her lips abruptly curved into a wide smile, her teeth showing more whitely than normal against the dust-laden skin of her face. 'You can do the cooking since you're the lady of leisure these days, and we'll probably be ready to drop—as usual—by the time the day's finished. Lord, it's been hot!' She wiped a forearm across her perspiring forehead as if to prove the point.

About to laughingly accede to the suggestion, Clancy suddenly found her reply being forestalled by her father declaring, 'I have a better idea. Why don't you all have dinner with us at the house instead?'

'Oh, that's very kind of you,' Lisa responded promptly with enthusiasm. 'I must admit I'd love to get away from the van for a change, and especially for a meal.' She hesitated, the beginnings of a doubtful frown creasing her forehead. 'Although I don't know about the fellers, though. They did say they were considering going in to town with a couple of their mates this evening.' She gave a ruefully expressive chuckle. 'That is, if they've still got the energy!'

Barrett smiled back understandingly. 'Well, the invitation's there if they would like to accept it, but you're most welcome to come, of course, even if they don't,' he assured her. 'Clancy or Ronan could drive down to collect you about seven, if that's all right with you.'

'Oh, yes—very,' Lisa accepted gratefully, and followed it with another eloquent half-laugh. 'I'm not sure my legs would have had sufficient strength left to carry me up there. We've been absolutely flat out since first light this morning and——' She broke off at a hailing shout from behind her, and after a quick look over her shoulder she made an apologetic moue. 'Sorry, but I'll have to go. The cartman's on his way again——' another hasty glance, succeeded by a grimace '—and so is Madeleine.' She was already turning away as she added swiftly, 'Thank you for the invite, Mr Sutherland, and I'll see you around seven.'

Lifting her hand in farewell, Clancy watched her friend start for the vines at a run, her gaze absently taking in Madeleine's figure as well . . . and her companion.

'Oh, there's Ronan!' Barrett exclaimed happily, and Clancy despaired when he immediately proceeded to attract the younger man's attention with a call and beckoned for him to join them. 'He must have left Isla's earlier than expected,' he appended in some surprise.

'Or perhaps she'd just forgotten he was coming,' suggested Clancy in uncontrollably satirical accents.

'Oh, no, nothing would make Isla forget when Ronan was going to visit her,' her father dismissed with a confident smile, the gibing note in her voice obviously escaping him. 'She thinks the world of him and would reschedule her whole day, or week if necessary, rather than miss seeing him.'

Just like every other female of his acquaintance, no doubt! derided Clancy to herself, surreptitiously watching Madeleine evidently doing her utmost to persuade her companion to disregard his employer's summons. Why, even Lisa, as she scurried back to work under Madeleine's censuring gaze, had still cast a susceptible glance his way, she recalled sourly, her lips levelling in a disgruntled fashion.

In fact, it had probably mainly been the thought of dining with Ronan that had led her friend to accept Barrett's invitation with such alacrity! After all, as Clancy well knew from past experience, when Lisa's interest in a man was fired, it wasn't readily extinguished.

Eventually, it appeared Madeleine's arguments had proved unsuccessful in preventing Ronan from attending his employer, although that didn't stop the dark-haired girl determinedly clinging to his arm as he approached, Clancy noted sardonically.

With an acknowledging nod and a pleasant smile for Madeleine, Barrett addressed his first remarks to his manager. 'You're back early. I didn't expect you until later this afternoon.'

Ronan raised a broad shoulder deprecatorily. 'Yes, well, we weren't the only visitors, unfortunately,' he relayed in a wry drawl, causing Clancy's stomach to lurch in a most incomprehensible manner.

We? Meaning himself and ... Madeleine? she pondered gloomily, and then immediately castigated herself soundly for even wanting to know. What did she care who had accompanied him, as long as *she* was relieved of his repressive presence? He deserved someone as malicious and self-centred as Madeleine!

It was that girl who Clancy suddenly realised was continuing in shrilly outraged tones, 'No, that miserable toad, Lucas, had to choose today to show up too ... for the first time in over a month! Heavens, what a perfectly repellent specimen he is! Like father, like son, I say!' Pausing, Madeleine patted her hair, visibly preening, her expression turning smug as her eyes connected briefly with Clancy's. 'Well, naturally Ronan didn't want me upset by any unpleasantness Luke might have instigated, so he considerately brought me home and I cooked us a delicious lunch here, didn't I?' She cast a coquettish glance at the man beside her for confirmation.

'Yes, it was very nice,' Ronan concurred—a trifle perfunctorily, Clancy thought—his gaze already having left Madeleine in favour of the man opposite. 'More importantly, however—do you need me for something?' he enquired of Barrett. 'Are there problems?'

'Well, not of a work nature,' Barrett replied with an unexpected hesitancy. 'It's just that... Well, I think I may have overdone it a little trying to show Clancy everything in one day, and I was wondering if you could take over from me for the rest of the afternoon.'

After a momentary spurt of surprise—he hadn't given any previous indication that he might be finding all their walking too much for him—Clancy immediately burst into hindering speech.

'You should have said! I don't mind waiting until another time.' The less she was in Ronan's company the better, in more ways than one, as far as she could see.

A sentiment that was obviously echoed by Madeleine as she hurried to insert, 'Yes, that sounds the best idea. It's what would have had to happen if we hadn't returned early, when all's said and done.' A current of asperity edged into her voice.

Ignoring both girls' interjections, Barrett merely waited for Ronan's response, his manner relaxing in seeming relief when the younger man shrugged and inclined his head briefly in acquiescence.

'If that's what you want,' he allowed, preparing to vault the fence between them, and Madeleine inhaled sharply with an angry hiss.

'But I had plans for this afternoon!' she protested furiously, her green eyes snapping. 'Why does it *have* to be today that she sees the place? I mean, it's not as if it's a matter of supreme importance!'

Not like her own plans were, assumed Clancy wryly, in spite of half agreeing with the dark-haired girl.

'No, although it is the second time already that an attempt's been made to show Clancy around,' put in Barrett quietly, but no less unwaveringly for all that. 'And since we'll be busy with irrigating tomorrow, and I don't know when it would be possible after that, I just thought that in view of the opportunity being available now...' He spread his hands expressively.

'Although if Ronan and Madeleine have something else planned...' Clancy offered excusingly. Notwithstanding Ronan's compliance, she was sure he had no actual wish to be her guide, as she also had no wish for him to be—especially after the last time.

'We haven't,' came the baldly abrupt denial from Ronan as he cleared the fence in one lithe, smooth action.

'But I did have!' Madeleine immediately reiterated in infuriated and aggrieved tones.

Ronan favoured her with an apologetic look. 'I'm sorry, but they'll keep until some other time, won't they?'

'It looks as if they'll have to,' she retorted ungraciously, and with a combination of a dismissive nod and a fulminating glare for the two beside him, she spun on her heel to take her evidently miffed departure.

'I'm sorry to have imposed on you, particularly on your day off,' it was Barrett's turn to apologise now to his manager as the three of them began making their way back along the rows of trees. 'But I did want Clancy to see everything today. It's just that I——'

Ronan cut him off with a shake of his head. 'It doesn't matter, and you're not imposing. I wasn't intending to stay much longer, anyway.'

Which remark had Clancy's lips pursing thoughtfully. All not so tied up on that front as Madeleine believed, or wanted, perhaps?

'You shouldn't have tried doing it all yourself if you weren't feeling up to it,' Ronan continued on a chiding note, sparing Clancy an accusing glance which promptly had her bristling at the arbitrary assumption that she was somehow to blame—as usual!

'Oh, no, I felt fine when we started,' Barrett hurried to assure him. 'It was just the last walk down to the Haighs' boundary that seemed to—er—get the better of me.' He uttered a rueful half-laugh, but to Clancy's mind with such unanticipated—self-consciousness?—that her curiosity was immediately piqued.

Could it possibly be that all their walking hadn't been too much for him, after all? That he had merely used it as . . . an excuse? That would, of course, explain why she hadn't noticed anything untoward prior to his first having mentioned it. But if that was the case, what on earth had been his reason? Her brows drew together in a frown as her brain worried at the question.

Not that Barrett had ever evinced any dislike of his neighbour's daughter, but if he was aware of her aspirations, and wasn't in favour of them, could it merely have been to spike Madeleine's guns? But no, she promptly discounted. To do that, he could simply have informed Ronan that there was something to do with the property that required his immediate attention. He hadn't needed to specifically request his manager to take his own place, unless . . .

The thought that now came to mind had Clancy almost gasping aloud and flicking a despairing look in Ronan's direction in an effort to gauge whether he had come to the same embarrassing conclusion. Neither his composed features nor his demeanour gave any clue, however, although that still couldn't stop a mortified flush from heating her cheeks. Oh, no, her father couldn't possibly be attempting to—*matchmake*...could he?

Was *that* the reason he had seemed to go out of his way to ensure they spent time together? It had more than surprised her on occasion, especially when she had believed that the sole reason for her being at Wattle Grove was supposedly in order to get to know him! At the time she had just put it down to Barrett's perhaps not being well enough to accompany her all the time, or that he didn't want her to think he was trying to completely monopolise her company, or even that, because he obviously thought so highly of his manager, he wanted her to get on well with him too...but not for the reason she was now beginning to suspect! That was just too humiliating, not to mention exasperating, to be endured!

Then again, just how did Ronan view the situation? she couldn't prevent herself from wondering. If that was Barrett's intent, was Ronan aware of it...and prepared to go along with it purely out of deference to his employer—just as she didn't doubt had been his reason for complying with her father's most recent request?

Of course, it would be the perfect way for him to effectively gain control of the whole of Wattle Grove on Barrett's death, the ungovernable thought immediately ensued. Or at least that was if, as he claimed, Barrett did indeed intend to leave part of the property to her. Even now she still found that idea inconceivable, not to say totally out of character.

Besides, what about Madeleine? Wasn't Ronan's interest—or his main interest, anyway, she amended scornfully—already engaged in that direction? She gave a dismissive shake of her head. No, as her numerous confrontations with Ronan surely attested, he had no more inclination to be drawn into any such plans her father might have than she did, and *she* very definitely meant to ensure no one had any doubts as to her feelings on that score! It was just damnably embarrassing, that was all.

Consequently, when they finally reached the house and she was left alone with Ronan once Barrett had continued on inside, Clancy promptly sought to make it plain she was no more in favour of Ronan being her guide than he undoubtedly was.

'Look, I'm sorry you were coerced into this, but really there's no need for you to give up your time for me,' she declared decisively. 'I'm quite capable of seeing anything else there is to see either on my own, or at some other time when Barrett feels more up to it.'

In response, Ronan's keen gaze appraised her briefly in unsettling detail. 'Except that Barrett obviously wanted you to be shown the rest of it today,' he stated in cool accents.

Clancy pressed her lips together. He wasn't making it any easier, and particularly when, for the last twenty-four hours, he had been the one avoiding her!

'And of course, I'd forgotten you always do *everything* he requests...no matter how unpalatable.' The gibe leapt from her lips before she could halt it.

'While you, on the other hand, will go to any lengths—no matter how perverse—to do precisely the opposite!' Ronan countered corrosively, making Clancy's jaw lift in fierce indignation.

'Perverse? Because I thought you might prefer spending your time in some other fashion? Stupid, maybe, it would appear, but hardly perverse, Ronan!'

He made a contemptuously disbelieving sound deep in his throat. 'Save that, I've no doubt, consideration of any kind had nothing whatsoever to do with it! More like it was just another convenient excuse for you to demonstrate your sheer bloody-mindedness where

Barrett's concerned.' He took an audible breath, his strong mouth shaping sardonically. 'Well, thank goodness I don't suffer from any such warped hang-ups. And I agreed that I *would* be your guide...today!' His fingers suddenly caught her in a grip that was like an iron-hard manacle about her wrist and began propelling her along beside him in the direction of the packing shed.

Clancy's temper flared, both at his words and his actions. 'Well, you were the one who withdrew from being my guide yesterday,' she reminded him on a sarcastic note. 'How was I to know you were any more willing today? And don't say, "Because I agreed to," because you did that yesterday too!'

Narrowed slate-blue eyes skimmed over her derisively. 'And maybe if you weren't so damned eager to disclaim everything connected with your father at every opportunity, I would have continued with it yesterday!

'Then you should at least be gratified that it meant I spent the whole of this morning in his company, as a result!' she sniped.

Ronan came to a standstill so abruptly that Clancy almost stumbled into him in surprise, her lips parting as she noted the unexpectedly suspicious and aggressively hostile look on his face.

'That is, unless *you* were also the cause of Barrett finding it too much to continue this afternoon!' he bit out in a voice of steel.

'No!' The vehement denial burst forth, her resentment disguising the spurt of relief engendered by the knowledge that at least he hadn't apparently come to the same conclusion as she had regarding Barrett's reason for making the request. 'In fact, he'd only just finished inviting my friends to the house for dinner this evening, and I doubt he'd have done that if I'd been making things difficult for him.'

'Unless he thought that the gesture might please you, and therefore possibly make you somewhat more amenable.'

Like a bribe! Clancy inhaled angrily. 'Except that I wasn't being difficult in the first place! Although even if I had been, I can assure you such a ploy would have failed.' She went on almost without pause. 'And will you let go of me?'—wrenching on her captive arm in a futile effort to break his grasp. 'I'm not some damned puppet to be continually pulled hither and thither at your whim!' Moreover, as they were much nearer the packing shed now there were other people about, and she felt a fool to be seen being towed along as if she were in disgrace.

'Although the idea does have a certain...appeal,' Ronan startled her by suddenly drawling in such an abrupt reversal of tone that she was thrown off balance.

Momentarily, she stared in disbelief at his amused expression, until a feeling of ungovernable aggravation gradually engulfed her at his habit of continually changing mood so that her emotions seemed always in turmoil. One moment she was resentful or infuriated, the next intimidated—but most vexing of all was the way in which he made her aware of him, of his overpowering masculinity, with every one of her senses...as now.

'If only for one of us, obviously!' she rejoined tartly at last, shaking free of him on feeling his grip relax. The ensuing shadow of a lazy smile that began to play across his lips only served to further increase her ire. 'Or was I just supposed to be so grateful you've apparently condescended to believe I wasn't the reason for Barrett's request that I'd welcome such attention?' Every word dripped with acid sarcasm.

His regard inscrutable, Ronan bent forward to crook a finger beneath her chin, lifting her face to his. 'I wouldn't ask that sort of question if I were you,' he recommended drily. 'I just might feel inclined to give you an answer... when we're somewhere less public.'

Clancy swallowed, her breathing quickening, and hastily moved back from his disturbing proximity. 'Then why don't you stop wasting time and just get on with showing me Wattle Grove?' she suggested stiffly on recovering her wayward senses and as much composure as she could manage.

'That's precisely what I was setting out to do—before you stopped me, darling... remember?'

Clancy clenched her teeth vexedly. Since she could hardly dispute the claim, there really wasn't much she could say. 'Then, after you,' she just managed to get out in an admirably restrained tone considering his taunting gaze was wreaking havoc with her determination to appear unaffected.

With a mocking inclination of his head, Ronan began leading the way, but although Clancy had intended her interest to be purely perfunctory—in order to have the tour completed as quickly as possible—she gradually found her attention becoming more and more absorbed, in spite of herself.

A machine separated the fruit into uniform sizes, but after that it was obviously the eyes of the human sorters that played the most important part in swiftly selecting and discarding any pieces considered not good enough for the market. And some of the reasons for their rejection were evident even to Clancy—the fruits had become marked from one cause or another, or weren't quite regular in shape—but there were also other pieces that suffered the same fate for no reason at all that she could see, and eventually it had her turning, if grudgingly, to Ronan for an explanation.

'What was wrong with that orange?' she leant closer to enquire with a frown. The noise from the sizing machine made it difficult to be heard from a normal distance. 'It looked all right to me.'

'Mmm, but that's because your eye isn't trained for the finer points,' he bent his head to explain with a smile. 'There's also a natural art to it. That's why not everyone has the ability to become a sorter, and why we retain those that do have the talent. While as to why that particular piece of fruit was discarded... it had too much skin.' Stretching forward suddenly, he removed another from the conveyor belt and handed it to her. 'While that one doesn't have enough juice.'

Clancy glanced at him askance, uncertain whether to believe him or not. The orange looked, and felt, perfect to her. 'But you can't tell that just by looking at it...can you?' she hazarded with a dubious half-laugh.

Ronan nodded, his lips quirking. 'It comes with practice, and knowing your fruit. You want me to prove it?' Taking the orange from her, he removed a pocket-knife from the pouch on his belt and proceeded to cut the fruit in two, then returned one of the halves to her while he sank his strong teeth into the flesh of the other.

Studying her own piece, Clancy supposed there could have been some room for improvement, although it was still considerably more juicy than some oranges she had bought on occasion, and certainly warranted better than being thrown away, as endorsed by her companion's action.

'What a pity it's not a judgement the everyday consumer can also make,' she commented with rueful feeling, following his lead and beginning to eat the tangy fruit.

'Although unnecessary if they purchase our brand, because we've already ensured they'll only receive the best,' put in Ronan subtly, tossing the peel into a nearby refuse bin.

'Point taken,' she conceded with a laugh, disposing of the remains of her own in similar fashion. 'I guess I'll have to keep my eye out for them in the supermarket when I return to Sydney.'

'Except that we don't supply to supermarkets. Ours is a first-quality eating fruit, fifty per cent of which goes to export, and the rest to airlines, ships, restaurants, high-class fruit shops, and the like. We produce to a standard, not a price.'

Clancy made a wry face. 'Then it's more than likely I couldn't afford them, anyhow.'

Ronan flexed a heavily muscled shoulder, his expression unexpectedly turning watchful. 'You could have them for free if you remained here.'

Clancy's breath caught in her throat. She had just started to relax with him, but now she could feel the nerves in her stomach beginning to contract unsettlingly again.

'You mean . . . p-permanently?' she stammered faintly in disbelief.

One dark eyebrow arched imperceptibly. 'Why not?'

'B-because my home's in Sydney.' Among other reasons!

He gave her a droll look. 'Although people do sell their homes and move elsewhere. Especially when there's nothing otherwise to keep them where they are.'

Clancy moistened her lips as confusion raged within her. Just why was he making such a suggestion? Because he believed Barrett wanted it? But her father had never so much as even hinted that that was what might be in his mind. Before now, he had never indicated that she might like to visit even! she reminded herself. No, Ronan was mistaken if he thought Barrett wanted her at Wattle Grove permanently.

As a result, she took a ragged breath and disputed, 'Nothing, that is, apart from friends, and a desire to continue living there.'

An ironic twist caught at Ronan's lips. 'Friends and a city taking precedence over family, as far as you're concerned, hmm?'

Clancy felt resentment flare. When had Barrett Sutherland ever been *family* to her? In any event...

'And you're wrong if you think Barrett would have it any other way,' she rejoined in uncontrollably bitter, but low, tones. She had no wish for anyone else in the shed to hear their conversation.

To her surprise, Ronan looked truly taken aback by that. 'And what's that supposed to imply?' he probed, frowning, and equally quiet-voiced.

Not wanting to discuss it further, and especially not where they were, Clancy shook her head. 'Nothing in particular.' And in the hope of distracting him, she went on immediately, 'Could we go on to the packing now, do you think?' that being the next process the fruit went through. 'I've always been interested to see how it's done,' she appended somewhat lamely with a nervous half-smile, but feeling she needed to add at least something.

Momentarily, as his intent gaze locked with her unconsciously pleading one, she thought he meant to ignore her attempted diversion, but then, with the smallest of shrugs, he seemed to relent, and a sighing breath of relief escaped her lips.

'Well, if you're really interested, the packing is done to specific patterns,' he advised in such a dry tone that Clancy couldn't control the colour that rose in her cheeks, 'each pattern being determined by the particular size of the fruit.'

Finding her interest actually becoming engaged now on watching the flying fingers of the packers as they wrapped each orange individually before placing them in their cartons, Clancy turned enquiring eyes upwards. 'For what reason?'

'Two very important ones,' Ronan returned with a wry quirk of his lips. 'Firstly, it enables the packers to know at a glance how many pieces of fruit they've packed without having to count them separately. And that's especially helpful when they might be packing two or three different sizes at any one time, or, because the fruit doesn't all come through in the one size, they have to leave a box half filled for a while.' He paused. 'The other reason is to stop the fruit from exploding.'

'Exploding!' Clancy's eyes widened in astonishment.

The tilt to Ronan's mouth became even more pronounced. 'Yes, with each carton weighing up to thirty kilos, when they're stacked for shipping like those——' indicating a pallet packed with boxes six high '—the fruit in the bottom cartons is under something like a hundred and fifty kilos of pressure, and if it isn't packed to its specific pattern then you've got trouble. Because if one piece of fruit gives way under the pressure, then so does the rest of the box, and when the box goes, down come the rest of the cartons—and *that* doesn't do much for your fruit, quite apart from the mess caused by the exploding carton.' He nodded towards the packers. 'Our way, the fruit can withstand up to four hundred kilos of pressure, and since we process in the vicinity of twenty million pieces of fruit a year, without ever having a carton explode...' He shrugged meaningfully, allowing their record to speak for itself.

Duly impressed, Clancy smiled. 'I'm beginning to see there's more to all this than meets the eye.'

'As there also is with some people,' Ronan concurred expressively, suddenly subjecting her to a searching contemplation which turned her mouth dry.

'Yes—well—thank you for showing me it all. I—I think I must have seen just about everything now,' she pushed out shakily, already turning for the wide front entrance. After their period, however brief, of something approaching accord, when she had started to relax in his company, she just didn't want it broken with more questions which she suspected would be forthcoming, and which she very definitely neither wanted to hear nor answer. Why couldn't he just leave things as they were? she despaired. With a manufactured laugh to cover her tension, she went on, 'No doubt I've already taken up more of your time than you can spare, what with all my questions. So...' She started walking away as quickly as she could without actually breaking into an ignominious run.

'And how about you allow me to decide how much time I can spare, huh?' Ronan's long-legged stride had him catching her effortlessly, to her agitated dismay. As he slid a hand beneath her hair, his fingers came to rest against the nape of her neck, sending tremors of unbidden and unwanted awareness chasing down her spine. 'Hell, you're acting as if you're scared to death of me!'

And why wouldn't she? She *was* apprehensive—of what his next unwarranted accusation concerning her attitude to her father might be, *and* of the thoroughly disastrous effect he had on her treacherous senses, in spite of everything!

Outside the shed now, Clancy couldn't meet his gaze and resolutely kept her eyes pinned on the horizon. But knowing she had to say something to forestall the ques-

tions she was fully expecting, she said the first thing that
sprang to her lips.

'Who's Lucas?' And her surprise at her query was no
less than Ronan's was. She had no idea what had
prompted the words, and could only presume the name
must have been lurking in her subconscious for some
reason ever since Madeleine had mentioned it.

'He's a cousin, by marriage. My aunt's stepson,' she
was informed perfunctorily. Although whether the
curtness was a result of her question, or due to his
cousin's character—as might be inferred from
Madeleine's remarks—she couldn't be certain. 'Why?'
he asked baldly.

Flustered, Clancy bit at her lip and shifted restively
from one foot to the other. 'I—I just wondered,' she
faltered uncomfortably. 'Barrett told me about your aunt
raising you, and——'

'Oh? And why would he do that?' he cut in before
she could finish.

Unsure of his mood, she chanced a surreptitious glance
upwards through the curtain of her long, sweeping lashes,
and was startled to find him appraising her in such a
lazy, lingering manner that her heart promptly skipped
a beat and her pulse raced.

Hastily looking away again, she murmured discomfitedly, 'I—er—happened to ask him who the Isla was
that you were visiting.' She drew a deep breath. 'I'm
sorry—I wasn't meaning to pry.'

She sensed rather than saw him shrug. 'There's no
harm done.' His fingers moved against her neck, where
they still rested, and disconcertingly she felt the effect
all the way down to her feet. 'I'll take you to meet her
some time, if you like.'

The offer was so casually made, and so unexpected,
that Clancy's eyes involuntarily flew up to his once more.

Why would he suggest taking her anywhere? They didn't even get along. Except for those occasions when they got along perhaps too well! a voice mocked inside her head, but which she steadfastly disregarded.

More importantly, why was she even considering the suggestion? For she was considering it, and willingly too, came the shocked admission. Lord, hadn't she learnt already that it was unwise to become involved with Ronan King? More to the point, why would she want to? His attitude was no different from her father's with regard to women! None the less, it seemed her subconscious wasn't interested in any such arguments as she suddenly found herself nodding in acceptance.

'Although...preferably when Lucas is absent,' she even ventured to quip, remembering Madeleine's comments regarding his relative.

Ronan laughed, a rich, vital sound that vibrated languidly through her nervous system. 'Most assuredly, when Lucas is absent,' he agreed.

'There's...discord between you?' she dared to hazard, struggling hard to regain control of her senses.

'There always has been,' he displayed no aversion to conceding. His mouth shaped wryly. 'Not that it causes me any lost sleep, but it makes it difficult for Isla, so—' expelling an expressive breath '—for her sake, these days I usually try to ensure he's not around when I visit, or, if he is, pre-empt the situation from becoming maybe too explosive by taking my leave.'

'He not feeling similarly beholden, for his stepmother's sake?' She suspected it would come very hard for someone of Ronan's rugged maleness to continually be the one to take the backward step. That he did, she could only deduce, evidently meant he thought as much of his aunt as she apparently did of him.

But now his eyes were shading with derision. 'I'm afraid there's only one person Lucas has ever felt beholden to—and that's himself! He's only interested in what suits him best, and how he can turn any given situation to his own advantage, no matter what the cost to anyone else.'

'I see.' She hesitated. 'I suppose living with someone like that while you were growing up must have made it even more difficult for you after—after your father left you as he did.' She began chewing at her lip, wondering if she had said too much.

Fortunately, though, Ronan's only response was a laconic, 'I survived.'

It gave her the courage, albeit after two steadying breaths, to put forward, 'But since the circumstances surrounding your father's—defection—weren't so very different from mine, why do you find it so impossible to understand my position concerning Barrett?'

Abruptly, all forbearance departed Ronan's expression, leaving it hard and daunting. 'Because I, at least, was willing to meet my father whenever he did attempt to contact me, which is a damned sight more than can be said for you!'

Clancy wrenched away from him, shocked by his sudden change, and furious at his accusation. 'And *if* Barrett had ever made an effort to contact me, maybe I would have done the same!' she flared.

'Oh, don't try playing the innocent with me, Clancy!' he scorned. 'I posted some of those letters Barrett sent you—and was made privy to their inhuman and discouraging replies!'

CHAPTER SEVEN

IN THE momentary silence that followed Ronan's grated retort, Clancy's shocked gasp was audible, her eyes huge in her whitening face. Then her breathing accelerated.

'Replies!' she reiterated derisively, fastening on to his last remark. 'There were no letters to answer! I don't know what supposed *replies*—' sarcastically stressed '—Barrett showed you, but I can assure you they weren't from me, because my father never wrote to me in his life!' Her glance turned ironic. 'So whatever he's told you, or shown you, was just fabrication. And, doubtless, solely for the purpose of creating the impression that *he* was the wronged party!'

A nerve along Ronan's jawline tensed. 'Oh, don't try pulling that one!' he blazed, the rasp of impatience laced with anger in his tone. 'Of course there were no replies—from *you*! You got your mother to do your dirty work for you.' A contemptuous curve shaped his mouth. 'But those letters were certainly no fabrications, posted to some fictitious address. They were sent to Tea-Tree Avenue all right, and that is where you live, isn't it? In Forestville?'

Clancy's lips parted. 'Well—yes,' she had no choice but to concur, albeit with a frown flickering across her brow. His claims didn't make sense! Her voice gathered strength almost immediately. 'But I never received any letters. And—and Barrett's lying if he says my mother wrote to him. Mum told me, many times, just how painfully obvious he made it that he wanted no more contact

127

with her immediately she informed him she was pregnant.' She made a dismissive gesture. 'No, Mum would never have written to him. Just the thought of his despicable treatment of her would have been more than sufficient to prevent her from lowering herself to such an extent.'

'Unless it conveniently provided her—and her equally vengeful daughter—with the opportunities to vent their petty spite, of course!' He shook his head in disgust. 'For heaven's sake, Clancy, for how long are you going to continue trying to deny it? Be honest enough to admit that much, at least. Can't you understand there's proof in the study right now—in the form of those very replies your mother allegedly never sent . . . in answer to those very letters you allegedly never received?'

For an instant, Clancy stood frozen into immobility as loyalty to her mother battled against what she was hearing. It wasn't true. It just couldn't be! Her mother had come to hate Barrett. There was no way she would have written to him, no matter what the reason. And—and besides, regardless of where her father's letters had supposedly been sent, didn't she herself know for a fact that they had never arrived? The timely reminder ensured it was loyalty to her mother that eventually won out.

'You're lying!' she denounced heatedly, her brown eyes flashing defiance. 'There is no——'

'You're the one who's lying!' Ronan broke in to counter on a biting, savage note. He smothered a violent expletive. 'But if it takes a visit to the study to finally put an end to your efforts to deny the undeniable . . .' Clamping his fingers about her elbow with bruising strength, he began hustling her towards the house.

Outwardly assured, but inwardly a mass of churning emotions, Clancy was too bewildered by the turn of events to even think of remonstrating with him for yet again forcing her to accompany him. Annoyance, bitterness, disbelief, even a faint, disconcerting curiosity—and a traitorous twinge of doubt, which vexingly she was unable to dispel—were all intermingling to make her mind whirl. He seemed so positive, and yet his so-called proof had to have been concocted... hadn't it?

Brief minutes later, as she stood in the study, her face blanching as she read the letters Ronan handed her—some many years old—she knew with an anguished contracting of her heart that they were no fabrication. Her mother *had* written to her father—a number of times, in fact—and, most wounding of all, apparently each time purportedly on Clancy's behalf.

To realise that her mother evidently had seen fit to intercept her mail was distressing enough, but that she should have replied, claiming such a variety of unfeeling reasons for Clancy not writing herself, was desolating. How could she have done such a thing? And particularly when she had so vehemently—and so constantly—maintained that Barrett was totally uninterested in their very existence.

It was more than obvious now that nothing could have been further from the truth—at least where his daughter was concerned—and pain-filled tears stung Clancy's eyes at the realisation. Why, on one occasion, when a previous invitation for her to visit him had been met with the dismissive claim that she was too young to travel that distance on her own and her mother and stepfather couldn't have afforded the expense anyway, it became apparent from her mother's wording that he had even offered to drive to Sydney to collect her in person in order to overcome such hindrances, but still her mother had thwarted any such contact. This time with the excuse that it wasn't convenient because Clancy had already made arrangements to stay with friends at the beach for those particular holidays. Only Clancy could never recall ever having had such a holiday, or a similar one even being proposed, if it came to that!

Feeling as if her whole life had suddenly been turned upside-down, Clancy trembled uncontrollably, thoughts of the sheer ill will involved in her mother's deceit sweeping over her in debilitating waves. Lord, had she really hated Barrett that much? So deeply, in fact, as to blatantly use her only child, and his, as a weapon against him by coldbloodedly foiling any communication, let alone contact, between them? Moreover, and what of *her*? the choking thought ensued. Her mother had been well aware just how her father's supposed renunciation of her had affected Clancy, especially in those early years. Or in her mother's desire to extract revenge, hadn't her daughter's feelings been considered of sufficient importance to even be taken into account? It appeared not.

By now Clancy's fingers holding the last and most recent of Estelle Munro's letters were shaking so badly her tear-washed gaze could only decipher the wavering words disjointedly. Nevertheless, she just managed to piece together the claim made on her behalf on this occasion that, now she had attained her majority, she had not the slightest interest in making her father's acquaintance and, as a result, would be grateful if he would refrain from harassing her with further attempts at communication because she had her own life to live.

Struggling to contain the sob that rose in her throat, she couldn't bring herself to read on—didn't want to, even—and she threw the letter on to the desk as if unable to bear touching it any longer.

'Well, what price all your denials now?' Ronan jeered, his voice harsh, brutal, jarring her already reeling senses.

It made him the focus for all her inner turmoil, thereby reminding her that he had been the cause of those devastating revelations and, in consequence, had her defensively venting her bitterness and despair on him.

'Oh, lord, I hate you! I hate you!' she choked brokenly, the sheen of her tears giving her eyes an almost fever-bright glitter. 'It was nothing to do with you! Why couldn't you have just left well alone?' Spinning on her heel, she fled towards the door—and nearly collided with Barrett as he entered the room.

'I thought I heard voices in here,' he began easily, and then frowned on registering Clancy's tearful and distraught features. 'Clancy...? What's wrong? What's upset you?' His voice turned urgent.

Clancy shook her head helplessly. 'Oh, Barrett... I'm s-so sorry,' she lamented in anguished tones.

'For what?' His confused glance switched anxiously to Ronan and back to her again. 'Will someone tell me what's been going on here?'

Casting a speaking look of her own in the younger man's direction, Clancy offered bitterly, if shakily, 'I'm s-sure Ronan will be only too pleased t-to do so. But if you will excuse me, I—I...' Her voice started to break, but, drawing on the last of her control, she mastered it and continued, 'I would rather talk to you later about it.' And without giving either of them a chance to delay her further, she hastily made good her departure—not only from their presence but from the house altogether.

She had to get away on her own for a while in order to at least make some effort to come to terms with what she had just discovered, and if she remained in the house there was more than a possibility she wouldn't be granted that time. And right at the moment she felt far too raw and lacerated by what she had learnt to want to talk to anyone—even Barrett.

Not really knowing, or caring, where she went, Clancy at last found herself at the river's edge and, sinking down on to the sun-warmed sand, she finally gave way to the scalding tears that had been pricking her eyelids for so long. Racked by sobs, she wrapped her arms about her midriff as engulfing waves of pain and sorrow swamped her.

After believing for so many years that her father had rejected her, to find now that her mother had been lying and, in fact, she had been the one deliberately keeping them apart, was almost too much to bear. Had her mother worried that any such contact might have altered Clancy's feelings towards herself? How could she *not* have known they wouldn't change? Wasn't it normal to relate to each of one's parents, without taking anything from the other?

Similar thoughts and questions, possible reasons and factors, went round and round like a top in Clancy's head until she felt dizzy with them—but still no real answers presented themselves.

Oblivious to the sun blazing down from the cloudless sky overhead and the piercing glare coming off the water, she stared unseeingly across the lazily moving river. She was just as unaware of the time passing, and it wasn't until the shadows created by the trees lengthened and deepened as the fiery red ball of the sun declined westwards that her surroundings gradually began to register. But only fleetingly even then, and only to make her stir restlessly in keeping with her despondent thoughts.

She still didn't feel ready to face anyone, let alone discuss the matter rationally—as she was sure Barrett would be anxiously waiting to do. So when Ronan suddenly and silently appeared from nowhere to calmly seat himself beside her, her first instinct was to flee once again.

'You can't run away from it forever, you know,' he proposed matter-of-factly, a hand on her arm successfully preventing her from rising when she would have scrambled to her feet. 'You have to face Barrett some time.' His fingers moved to cup her chin, turning her head towards him. 'When you disappeared for so long he really started to worry about you.'

Clancy bit her lip, all resistance draining from her at his words—and his unexpectedly gentle voice. She felt too weary mentally, if not physically, to continue her effort to escape, anyway.

'So he sent you to look for me,' she surmised on a sigh, veiling her eyes with her lashes.

'No. We both set out to find you. I just happened to be the one who knew you'd been here before.' A faint touch of humour tinged his voice and, suddenly realising precisely where she was—and what had occurred there—Clancy jerked away from his touch, hot colour ebbing and flowing beneath her satin-smooth skin.

'It was simply somewhere quiet and—and private,' she defended protectively, dropping her gaze to her restively entwining fingers which were laced about her updrawn knees.

Ronan nodded. 'I guessed as much.' There was a pause, and then he exhaled heavily. 'You weren't aware Barrett had been writing to you all that time, were you?'

At last he understood! None the less, in spite of all the comments she could have made—felt entitled to

make—all she could manage was a dismal shake of her
head and a barely audible, 'No.'

'Mmm, from what Barrett's just said, apparently he'd
begun to suspect that could perhaps have been the case,'
he revealed quietly. Pausing again, he ran a hand around
the back of his neck. 'I'm sorry for having given you
such a hard time about it, but I was under the impression
that——'

'It doesn't matter,' she broke in on a husky whisper.
'It appears everyone was labouring under the wrong
impression...ex-except for my mother.' Her lips trembled
as uncontrollable tears started to her eyes once more and
streaked her face before she could hastily wipe them
away.

Watching her, Ronan uttered a stifled groan. 'Oh,
hell!' Catching her to him convulsively, he smoothed a
tanned hand over her tawny hair in slow, commiserating
movements. 'It's really turned you inside out, hasn't it?'
he said heavily against her temple. 'Maybe you were
right. I should have let sleeping dogs lie.'

Although that had been her own initial reaction,
Clancy now found herself shaking her head, albeit
weakly, in contradiction. Perhaps it was simply because
his deep voice was soothing, a balm to her troubled spirit,
and their previous confrontations at least temporarily
laid aside. For whatever reason, though, she only knew
his nearness, the strength and warmth of his strongly
muscled body, was somehow comforting, and she was
content to remain resting against him, her head unconsciously burrowing closer into the curve of his shoulder.

'No, that wouldn't have been fair to Barrett,' she disputed on a softly expelled breath. 'He deserves to have
it known that he did at least try to contact me.' She
chewed at her lower lip. 'I just don't know how he could

have wanted anything to do with me—let alone invite me to stay here—in view of the way he must have believed *I'd* rejected him all these years.'

The curve of Ronan's mouth became wry. 'Then you still don't understand your father very well. Not only is there not an ungenerous bone in his body, but his only child has always meant a great deal to him. And since this seemed likely to be his only, and possibly last chance to actually speak to you in person, as far as he was concerned there was nothing he wouldn't have done if it meant the two of you at least spending some time together.' He lifted a muscular shoulder. 'Besides, as I said, apparently he'd already begun to have some misgivings regarding the veracity of your mother's letters, in any case.'

Clancy tilted her head back to see him better, a frown furrowing her forehead. 'For any particular reason?'

His eyes, a deep and dark grey, looked down at her as he rubbed his jaw thoughtfully. 'I gather it was due to the last one mostly. He seemed to feel that, since you were certainly of an age by then to do your own writing, your supposed wish for him to refrain from harassing you with further attempts at communication would have carried far more weight, and been considerably more effective, if it had been penned by yourself.'

Suddenly aware of the intensity of his gaze—it was the first time since their disconcerting meeting that night in the orchard that she could remember his blue-grey eyes being that particular soft and sensuous colour when they rested on her—Clancy felt her breath catch in her throat and she glanced away quickly as a shock wave of warmth spread through her.

'I—I suppose so,' she pushed out unsteadily. Determinedly forcing herself to concentrate, she went on,

'Then why didn't he come to Sydney and—and try to make contact with me in person?'

Ronan gave a short, mirthless laugh. 'He'd already tried that on a couple of occasions. How did you think he came by that photo of you in the study?'

In actual fact, his original mention of it had slipped her mind, and since coming to live at Wattle Grove she'd had too many other things to think about. But as she recalled, from the background and what she was wearing in the photograph, she guessed it must have been taken when she was about eleven or twelve and just arriving home from school.

'I did wonder,' she owned slowly. Then, more swiftly, 'But if he was close enough to take a photo, why on earth didn't he speak to me—explain who he was?'

Ronan's mouth levelled. 'Because your mother refused to allow it. She claimed, among other things, that it would undermine your feelings for your stepfather, and that you were still too young to deal with such a traumatic encounter.' He uttered a disparaging sound. 'She said it would be better if he waited until she'd had more time to prepare you for the meeting. While as for Barrett... Well, he says he did consider ignoring her, but being the person he is eventually, if extremely reluctantly, he decided against doing so, just in case she was right. In which case, it could have ended up doing more harm than good, and having entirely the opposite result to the one he was hoping for.' Pausing, he released an expressive breath. 'So he contented himself with a few photographs, and the hope that one day, some day, the situation would change for the better.'

Clancy nodded sadly, her heart going out to her father, imagining just how devastated she would feel at being denied access to any child she might have—illegitimate or not. In an effort to dispel the distressing thought, she slanted a half-quizzical, half-disbelieving glance upwards.

'And you still managed to recognise me from a photo *that* old?'

A lazy smile spread across Ronan's features, deceptively vital, and dangerously beguiling. 'Your hair's the same,' he declared, toying with a sun-streaked strand close to her cheek, and making her breathing ragged. 'And so are those beautiful velvety brown eyes.' His voice deepened to a husky pitch. 'As also is that tip-tilted nose——' stroking a forefinger down its length '—and...that sultry, so very kissable mouth.' He grazed a thumb slowly across her lower lip and his touch burned like fire against the sensitive skin.

'Y-you're sure you're describing the right p-person?' she attempted to quip in an effort to lighten the abruptly stifling atmosphere, but her tone was too breathily uneven for it to be successful, and Ronan's eyes, the smoky grey of smouldering wood fires, grew dusk-dark and sleepy as they caught hers and held.

'Very sure,' he murmured resonantly, and before she could even think to demur he bent his head, and the sculptured warmth of his mouth found her parted lips with a sensual intimacy that suspended her breathing.

Clancy immediately felt a wave of heat envelop her as his tongue explored and tasted the honeyed lining of her mouth, searching out her most responsive areas and sensuously stimulating them until her lips were clinging unreservedly to his and her tongue feverishly entangling with his own.

Compliantly, she allowed him to draw her closer, his arms moulding her tightly against his hard, lean length, fitting them together as if by design, and she couldn't gainsay the heavy ache that started in her stomach and progressed downwards. With a helpless moan she raised her arms to encircle his neck.

Ronan shuddered, his breath coming unsteadily as he lowered her to the sand, supporting her head on his arm. His lips moved along the delicate line of her jaw to her ear, and she quivered as his tongue proceeded to leisurely trace the shell-like contours. Then his mouth was assaulting the rapidly beating hollow of her throat, the silky skin of her tanned shoulder exposed by her knitted-cotton tube top, one hand sliding down her body to her waist, her hip, and then back again to cradle a swelling breast.

Clancy's lips parted, her breathing becoming laboured. Every nerve was taut, responsive, her senses whirling at his sure touch. Instinctively, she strained against him, luxuriating in the virile, masculine strength of him, the broad chest wherein she could feel his heart beating as heavily as her own.

Lightly Ronan brushed her nipple against his thumb until it hardened to a throbbing crest that surged against the thin material of her top, and she was aware of a quickening inside her. He was stirring a yearning, a craving for more, she was powerless to control, and her fingers tangled frantically within his dark hair, pulling him closer, urging his mouth back to hers.

And with sensuous thoroughness he complied. His lips closed on hers hungrily, his teeth nibbling at her lips, suction erotically drawing her tongue into the warm moistness of his mouth, his possession complete and overwhelming.

Shaken by the intensity of feeling he was arousing, Clancy clung to him dazedly, unaware his hand had performed a different task until his mouth trailed a searing path from her arched throat to her now naked breasts. Full, and aching with need, they swelled voluptuously at the gentle rotation of an enlarged nipple between forefinger and thumb, and with a low groan Ronan circled it with his tongue and lips in heated urgency.

Clancy shuddered, desire spiralling through her as white-hot rivers of pleasure radiated outwards from the focal point of his rhythmically suckling mouth. She knew she should protest, but the moist flicking of his tongue, and the fierce pull of his lips, were nearly sending her out of her mind, and when the fire he was igniting in her blood moved lower, deeper into her stomach, she was defeated by her own treacherous longings, burning with a hunger she had never before known.

She tried to tell herself it was merely reaction to those earlier shocking disclosures, an outlet for her already overcharged emotions. But, no matter what reasoning she employed, it still didn't satisfactorily explain away the unbridled desire she was experiencing. And it was desire—hot, throbbing, and consuming—she acknowledged shakily.

She *wanted* him to make love to her! It was as simple as that. Wanted him to continue what he was doing, wanted to feel the heat and texture of his bare skin against hers. And, yes, wanted him buried deep within her with a fundamental need that shocked her with its so very physical basis.

But when Ronan turned his attention to her other breast all coherent thought was erased from her mind and, blind with need, she unbuttoned his shirt with trembling fingers and pushed it from his shoulders. With a sigh of satisfaction she slid her hands savouringly upwards across his hair-roughened chest, around his ribs to his back, discovering how marvellous his body felt, and revelling in the feel of the hard muscles rippling beneath her sensitive fingertips, the sense of latent power that lay just under his coppered, satin skin.

Ronan tensed at her caressing explorations, a low, painful groan, as if he were undergoing torture, emanating from deep in his chest before shuddering upwards as he raised his head to gaze down at her with dark and turbulent eyes.

'Dear lord, I'm only flesh and blood, Clancy,' he warned hoarsely.

Unable to prevent herself, she leant forward to caress the warm skin of his throat with lips and tongue. 'Mmm, glorious flesh and blood,' she breathed in thickened accents, and with a strangled sound he crushed his mouth to hers, the hair on his hard chest arousingly abrading the swollen tips of her breasts as he possessively pinned her beneath him.

Clancy's senses were filled with his taste and earthy male scent, her whole world reduced to nothing but the feel, the touch, the stimulating weight and warmth of him.

Now, the arm she was lying against curled tightly about her shoulders, Ronan's other hand moving urgently over her curving form from shoulder to waist, then lower to gently flaring hip and the slender length of tanned thigh exposed by her denim shorts. And when his fingers slid under the rumpled folds of her top to splay across her taut stomach, Clancy quivered, her own hands clutching at his back, and then feverishly kneading the long, firm muscles when his fingers slipped lower, beneath the waistband of her shorts.

Her body on fire, she arched to meet him... and then stiffened as a calling voice abruptly forced its way through the mind-drugging sensations engulfing her.

'Clancy! Ronan! Are you down this way?' Barrett's anxious voice came from behind them, and sounding closer with each step.

With a gasp, Clancy pushed herself into a sitting position, fumbling to right her clothing as cold, numbing reason made its shattering return. Chills raced across her skin—even as her cheeks burnt hotly—at the thought of what she had nearly allowed to happen.

Unable to look at him, let alone speak, she left it to Ronan to answer her father's call as he repaired the state of his own clothing. Nevertheless, she was still very much aware of him, of the rough unsteadiness of his breathing which matched her own, but when he would have drawn her into his arms—to kiss her one last time, she suspected—she pulled away from him sharply.

'No!' The word emerged more fiercely than she intended. Since the episode obviously would have been nothing more than a self-indulgent diversion for him— how could she have forgotten Madeleine so heedlessly?—she didn't want him thinking it had affected her any more significantly. 'I—I mean, Barrett's almost here,' she stammered, trying to camouflage her mistake.

An oblique tilt caught at Ronan's mouth. 'Although somehow I doubt he would have any objections,' he drawled.

Implying that he too had suspicions that her father might be attempting to matchmake? she speculated in mortification. And before she could recover, she suddenly found herself swept into his arms and his lips claiming hers in a savouring, lingering kiss that sent a pervasive warmth coursing through her, despite all her efforts to remain unaffected.

By the time Ronan released her, Barrett was just nearing the head of the beach, and, even further chagrined and horrified by her latest unfathomable response to Ronan, Clancy immediately turned in her father's direction. She didn't know if he had witnessed that last embrace, but right at the moment she didn't much care. She only knew she needed time, and some distraction—*any* distraction—in order to regain control of her shamefully unruly emotions.

'Ah, you found her,' Barrett said to the younger man with evident relief, but with his dark brown gaze remaining fixed concernedly on Clancy, as if attempting to gauge the state of her feelings. 'You're all right?' he asked her softly as he approached. 'We were worried about you. Especially when we couldn't find you.'

Clancy bit her lip, his words suddenly reminding her of the reason she had sought the haven of the river in the first place. 'Yes, I'm—all right,' she answered on a somewhat husky note, taking an involuntary step towards him. 'And I'm sorry if I worried you. I didn't mean to. It was just that—that . . .'

All of a sudden there was a lump in her throat, making it impossible for her to continue, and when Barrett silently opened his arms to her, it seemed the most natural thing in the world for her to walk straight into them, unbidden tears starting afresh when his arms closed around her and she laid her head against his shoulder. Her emotions *were* working overtime! she thought with lachrymose ruefulness.

'It doesn't matter, love, it doesn't matter,' her father repeated like a comforting litany, his hand smoothing over her hair. 'You're here now. That's all I care about.'

Clancy brushed her fingertips across her wet lashes. 'But it was such a—a . . .' She hesitated, pressing her lips together, reluctant to put it into so many words. 'It was such a spiteful thing to have done—to both of us,' she managed to push out diffidently at last, and she felt Barrett's chest rise and fall heavily as he expelled a deep sigh.

'More to you than to me, I suspect, since I had already begun to surmise what Estelle was doing,' he acceded in weighty tones. 'I knew it wasn't my wish for us never to know one another, whereas you didn't.'

'But—why?' She lifted bewildered eyes to his, a rich dark brown, and so very like her own. 'Why was she so determined that I believe you had deserted the pair of us without so much as a second thought?' She paused, swallowing hard and painfully. 'Because it was only when she became pregnant—that you informed her you were already married?'

Barrett's sharp intake of breath was audible as he suddenly grasped her by the shoulders, holding her slightly away from him and gazing down at her with unexpected grimness. 'Is that what she told you?' he demanded in rasping tones of disbelief, and she gave a faltering nod. *'The bitch!'* The succinct epithet burst from his throat with such uncharacteristic fury that Clancy blinked. Normally, he was such a mild-mannered, softly spoken man that it somehow made his present grated denunciation all the more potent by contrast. With an obvious effort, he recovered his composure and raised a hand to graze her cheek in an apologetic gesture as he went on in more customary accents, 'I'm sorry. In spite of her behaviour, she was still your mother, and I'm sure you wouldn't appreciate me describing her in such a fashion. None the less...' He pulled at an earlobe and let out a heavy breath. 'I do think it's past time you and I had a long talk. Evidently there's quite an amount of clearing up that needs to be done.' His expression turned rueful.

'Or are you now doubtful that my version of events will be any more truthful than Estelle's apparently was?'

Clancy worried at her lower lip with even white teeth. There was that possibility, she supposed, and with her mother now unable to deny any claim he might make . . . She sighed. Despite her mother's behaviour—at best, unkind, at worst, plain malicious—she still felt a strong sense of loyalty, of sympathy, towards her that couldn't—wouldn't—be denied.

After all, Estelle Munro *had* made a home for her and cared for her all those years, even though perhaps not all the assertions she had made during that time had been as accurate as she wanted her daughter to believe. But then, maybe she had considered she had good reason for doing so. She had to have had some right on her side, didn't she? Clancy shook her head in confusion.

'I don't really know,' she answered at last with painful honesty. 'I guess the best I can offer is that I'll try and keep an open mind.'

'And that's all I ask.' Barrett's satisfaction with her reply was obvious. Then, with a wry half-smile, 'Although I'm afraid our talk is going to have to wait a little longer, just the same. What with everything that's happened, it's probably slipped your mind, but your friends were invited to dine with us this evening and it will soon be time for them to be collected.'

Clancy gasped in dismay. 'Oh, lord, I had forgotten all about that,' she admitted.

Momentarily, she debated suggesting the invitation should be transferred to another night, but knowing what Lisa would think of that proposal finally dissuaded her against it. If her friend was so anxious to vie with Madeleine for Ronan's attention—which she didn't doubt was Lisa's intention and wish—wasn't that to her own advantage at the moment?

It might allow her to attain some detachment, to ignore him, and thereby perhaps overcome the memories of her own recent errant behaviour as well which were disconcertingly returning to plague her as gradually she became aware of Ronan's presence once more.

CHAPTER EIGHT

IRRESPECTIVE of her hopes of ignoring Ronan, however, as the evening progressed Clancy discovered, disquietingly, that such an idea was far easier to conceive than to put into practice.

The trouble was, there was a magnetism in the man, a force and vitality, that made it impossible to disregard him. By his mere presence he seemed to draw her attention, and despite her best efforts to concentrate on those other males present—Darrell and Warwick having accepted the invitation, after all—deep down she knew that it was only pretence.

In truth, she was always aware of him, instinctively and intensely aware of every move he made and every word he spoke—and particularly so whenever Lisa was involved. Which was quite a considerable amount of the time, Clancy was vexed with herself for noting. But having been afforded the chance to show her interest in Ronan at last, Lisa had made it plain right from her arrival that she intended to make the most of the opportunity.

And as she surreptitiously watched her friend go about attempting to monopolise Ronan in her most sparkling and flirtatious manner, Clancy found herself becoming more and more irritated by the sight, a tight knot lodging in her chest every time Ronan responded to the other girl's coquettish behaviour.

It wasn't that she begrudged her friend her chance to engage Ronan's interest, she assured herself staunchly.

When all was said and done, only this afternoon hadn't she been counting on just that happening, to enable herself to remain detached? No, indeed, it wasn't on her own behalf she was feeling so tense and dissatisfied. She was merely annoyed by her friend's flagrantly transparent conduct, and apprehensive that Lisa might be hurt in the outcome, that was all.

As a result, when Darrell and Warwick reluctantly brought the visit to an early close because of the long and busy, and naturally hot, day they anticipated on the morrow—Lisa's disappointed pouts making it evident she would have been prepared to stay all night, regardless, noticed her friend with uncustomary bitchiness—it was Clancy who offered with enthusiastic alacrity to drive them back to their van. Although purely for Lisa's sake, in order to stop her either making more of a fool of herself, or conversely being made a fool of, of course!

'No, Ronan can take them,' countered Barrett casually, all unaware, but bringing a satisfied smile back to Lisa's face, at least. 'And while he's gone I'll help you to clear up and put everything away.' He chuckled. 'You do it so much more neatly than we do.'

'Oh, we can stay and help with that before we leave,' Lisa promptly offered from suspect motives, already eagerly turning back from the doorway.

'No, no, don't you worry about it,' Barrett vetoed, ushering her towards the door once more. 'You need your sleep, with the work you're doing. There's not that much to do, and we'll have it finished in no time, won't we, Clancy?'

What could she say? With as much good grace as she could muster, she gave a nod and a weak half-smile in resigned confirmation.

A short while later, with their work concluded—
although without Ronan having yet returned, Clancy
noticed in mounting protest she had no reason to experience—Barrett slanted her a partly smiling, partly
hesitant glance.

'Well, now that's out of the way, shall we make our-
selves a cup of coffee and—er—have our talk?' A pause.
'Or would you prefer to wait until tomorrow?'

As much as Clancy was tempted to procrastinate—she
really wasn't sure she was in the right frame of mind for
any more revelations at the moment—eventually she
allowed on a sighing note, 'No, tonight's fine.' Hesi-
tating herself now, she moistened her lips. 'I guess the
sooner I know the whole story, the sooner I'll be able
to come to terms with it. At least—I hope so. Because
to date...' She made a helpless gesture. But when he
would have offered some sympathy, she shook her head
and forced a wry smile. 'No, I'm all right. Just a trifle
confused, I suppose.' She turned away to begin ex-
tracting cups and saucers from a cupboard. 'You go on
into the sitting-room and I'll bring in the coffee in a
minute,' she proposed, and after a moment's doubtful
contemplation of her tautly held figure, Barrett did as
suggested.

Nevertheless, when she joined him presently with their
coffee and took the seat he indicated on the sofa next
to him, Barrett took hold of one of her hands between
both of his own to exhort urgently, 'Look, it doesn't
have to be tonight if you don't feel you're ready. I can
imagine how difficult it is for you; how upsetting it has
been already.' He gave her a reassuring smile, albeit one
tinged with sadness. 'I do understand, you know, how
hard it must be for you to accept me as your father in
view of what you've apparently been told by Estelle, but

I would like us to be friends, at least, in time, if that's possible, and—' his forehead creased worriedly '—forcing you to hear facts you may not feel ready to accept...' He exhaled heavily. 'Well, I don't want it to have the opposite effect, and, rather than bringing us closer together, drive you further away instead. As I said earlier, I do realise your feelings must still lean towards your mother, and I hope you'll believe me when I say it's not my wish to destroy the feelings you have for her——'

'And as *I* said, I'll try to keep an open mind,' she interrupted to remind him softly. Why, he was as nervous about this as she was! she had suddenly realised, and unconsciously her fingers returned the comforting pressure of his. Then, drawing a deep breath, she plunged in resolutely to take the initiative. 'So—from your reaction this afternoon, I take it that—that it wasn't only *after* she became pregnant that Mum discovered you were married?'

Barrett shook his head. 'Because there never was any such discovery *to* make!' he declared with an obviously uncontrollable trace of harshness. 'She was well aware from our very first meeting, on the day she started working here, that I was married.' There was a brief hesitation before he qualified with determined honesty, 'And happily so, I might add.'

A frown drew Clancy's brows together at his last statement. 'Then, if that was the case, why did you— why did you...?'

'Have an affair with Estelle?' His lips compressed, then before answering he handed her her coffee from the table in front of them, and took a mouthful of his own as he subsided against the back of the sofa. 'It was never my intention to, originally. It was just that ... Oh, hell, I know I'm not blameless—far from it—but she made it so damned hard to refuse!' he groaned. 'No matter where I went, whichever way I turned, she was always there, flirting, making it obvious she was more than willing. And she was an attractive, lively girl in those days, while I . . .' He bent his head. 'I was thirty-nine, with all the normal sexual urges . . . and a beautiful, courageous wife, heaven rest her soul, who'd been severely crippled with multiple sclerosis for all but the first year of our eleven-year marriage.'

Involuntarily, Clancy's heart went out to him. 'And so the inevitable occurred,' she surmised quietly, trying to come to grips with the picture of her more often than not bitter mother as lively and flirtatious.

'And so the inevitable occurred,' he conceded on a sighing note. 'We had an affair which lasted for about three months. An affair I've regretted ever since. Oh, not for what it produced!' came the hasty and earnestly voiced disclaimer. 'You were the only good thing to come from the whole sordid mess.' A hint of moisture was apparent in his eyes as he touched a hand to her cheek affectionately. 'Would I have supported you financially all these years if I'd thought otherwise?'

Clancy's hand shook so violently she had to deposit her cup on the table before the coffee in it spilt. 'Y-you supported me?' she just succeeded in pushing out in strangled tones, her face ashen.

His face only a little less pale than hers as he realised her ignorance of the matter, Barrett swiftly deposited his cup beside hers and caught hold of both her hands tightly.

'Oh, hell, I'm sorry, love. I should have guessed that if Estelle hadn't told you about the letters, then doubtless she wouldn't have told you of the money either.' He frowned. 'Although surely you must have seen some reference to the payments when you went through her and Ron's papers after they died?'

Clancy gave the barest shake of her head, outwardly numb, but inwardly her thoughts and emotions in anguished turmoil. No wonder her mother and stepfather had appeared to manage their money so well! They'd had outside assistance. And judging, with new insight now, what they had achieved, some considerable assistance, at that, too!

A shiver of despair and a mounting sense of outrage rippled through her. Dear lord, had there been *any* truth in her life? She wanted to scream, to vent her resentment, to demand answers . . . but her mother was no longer available to give those answers, and so her anger involuntarily became focused on the only person who was.

'And was that her pay-off, to induce her to leave Mildura? Or a salve for your conscience?' she gibed acrimoniously, snatching her hands free.

An expression of pain crossed Barrett's face. 'Neither,' he denied heavily. Then, with his voice becoming more forceful, 'No matter what you may think now, I only wanted what was best for you. Good grief, I would have raised you myself, here at Wattle Grove, if it had been at all possible, but——' his voice lowered to a grieving tone once more '—knowing the added hurt and distress that would have caused Judith, how could I? I think the greatest pain her affliction ever caused her was always the knowledge that she wasn't able to provide us with the children we'd both wanted so much.'

Clancy steeled herself against any unbidden feelings of compassion. 'Then perhaps it would have been better for all concerned if you'd given a little more thought to that before indulging your baser instincts!'

'You think I don't know that?' He closed his eyes momentarily in despair. 'But unfortunately it's always easiest to be wise *after* the event! How was I to have known Estelle...?' He came to a jaw-clenching halt, making a dismissive gesture with one hand.

'Oh, please, don't bother to make any belated efforts to spare my feelings now,' Clancy immediately prompted on a sardonic note. 'What else is there that could possibly shock me more than I have been already? I mean to say, I may only have been the ham in the sandwich in this whole sorry business, but—*just for once*—I really would like to be told the whole, plain, unadulterated truth...if that's not too much trouble, of course!'

Barrett gave a regretful shake of his head, but instead of answering, entreated urgently in lieu, 'Don't let it make you bitter like your mother, Clancy...please! I think I would rather we'd never met at all than to have that happen.'

'And maybe it would have been best, at that,' she snubbed, and felt a stab of guilt at the look of sorrow that shadowed his eyes. She knew she was acting vilely— and even probably unfairly as well, where he was concerned—but she couldn't seem to help herself. It was as if her turbulent emotions were determined to find release any way they could.

'You—really mean that?'

The slight break in his voice had Clancy dropping her gaze to her tightly entwined fingers in her lap. Was that what she really would have preferred? she probed her feelings restlessly. To go through life never having met her father, blindly believing all her mother had said about him, never learning the actual truth—even if it was painful?

'Do you, Clancy?' prompted Barrett with a heart-wrenching sadness that brought tears welling into her eyes, and she shook her downbent head slowly.

'I'm sorry,' she began in a small, choking voice. 'I sh-shouldn't be taking it out on you, but——'

'I'm the only one here, hmm?' he inserted, an understanding smile touching his lips as he tilted her misty-eyed features up to his.

Clancy sighed and nodded. 'I'm sorry,' she said again, but this time it was her father who gave a negating shake of his head.

'No, if there's any apologising to be done, it should be by others, not you.' He made a sound of self-disgust. 'Maybe if I'd done things differently in the beginning—made a more determined effort to see you, not allowed Estelle to dictate the terms so much...'

Clancy moistened her lips. 'But if Mum knew you were already married, why didn't she take precautions against becoming pregnant?' she puzzled. 'I mean, reliable contraceptives were available then, and she must have realised there was a likelihood of such a thing happening.' Her mother might have contended she'd been taken advantage of, but never once had she claimed to have been ignorant of the facts of life.

'Yes—well...' Barrett exhaled a long breath, running a hand through his greying hair. 'Except that I suspect it was always her intention to use any such pregnancy as a means of forcing me to divorce Judith and marry her instead,' he disclosed carefully, and Clancy's throat constricted.

'"Was always her intention",' she repeated, swallowing. 'Implying, she did—actually try—something of the sort?'

He nodded heavily. 'As well as threatened to inform Judith of the whole story when the ploy failed to work.' His lips twisted. 'Fortunately, I was able to dissuade her from that course by making her see that, once Judith knew, then there would be no reason for me not to apply for custody of the child, and it soon became apparent she didn't want that at any price.' An ironic half-smile shaped his mouth. 'Little did I realise, though, that future revenge might have had a bearing on her attitude—as seems likely from her later behaviour. By deliberately portraying me in the worst possible light, she must have thought there'd never be any likelihood of our forming any kind of relationship if, by some strange chance, we did eventually happen to meet. A hoped-for relationship she knew only too well meant a great deal to me. The more so, even, after Judith died.' Pausing, he eyed her speculatively. 'And in that regard, considering the claims she evidently had made about me, I guess, by rights, I could have expected some pretty harsh words from you when we did finally meet.'

Twin circles of colour stole into Clancy's cheeks. 'Yes—well—I must admit I did have some thoughts along those lines when I arrived,' she owned self-consciously.

'Yet you didn't express them.'

'I found *thinking* of denouncing someone was quite different again from actually doing so to their face,' she supplied with a wry grimace. 'Besides, since I believed you'd never shown any interest in me, I was determined to do the same concerning you, and thus prove it meant nothing to me, anyway.'

'Then why did you think I asked to see you that first day?'

Clancy looked away. 'I thought it most probable that you'd been forced into it. To put on an act, for Ronan's benefit, simply because he'd recognised me from that photo in the study.'

'Oh, no!' Barrett despaired, squeezing her shoulder in a sympathetic gesture. 'How resentful you must have felt. And all I can say is, thank heaven you didn't allow those feelings to prevent you from coming altogether.'

'Except that, as I recall, your manager had somewhat more to do with that than I did,' she returned in eloquent tones.

'That's right, you did mention something similar at the time,' he averred, lips twitching a little. 'And in view of what's transpired since, I guess I have even more cause now to be thankful he—er—ensured your presence that afternoon.'

She too, Clancy supposed, although nothing on earth would have made her admit as much. The reference to the other man did, however, prompt the realisation that he hadn't as yet returned from driving her friends back to the van. Then, berating herself for even noticing, she purposely reverted to their former topic.

'Although you haven't yet told me exactly how my stepfather fitted into all this,' she reflected, eyeing him quizzically. 'You commented this morning about my grandmother saying something to the effect of Mum's not having been true to him?'

Barrett nodded. 'Mmm. Ron had been dating Estelle for almost a year before she came to work at Wattle Grove. He'd even asked her to marry him, I understand, but she'd refused. With an eye always on the main chance, I gather she was . . . well, looking for bigger fish

to fry, shall we say? And that was when Ron left Mildura
and moved to Sydney. Then when Estelle finally realised
I wasn't going to divorce Judith, she evidently decided
Ron Munro could be of use to her, after all, and armed
with my offer of support for you she set off after him.'
He raised an expressive shoulder. 'The rest you already
know.'

Clancy touched her teeth to her lower lip thoughtfully. She wasn't surprised by what she had just heard.
In truth, she wondered if anything would ever surprise
her again after the disclosures she had been subjected to
that day! And as it happened, her father's explanation
had merely served to confirm what she had always suspected. That Ron Munro's feelings for his wife had never
really been reciprocated.

'It's not a pretty picture, is it?' she mused now with
a sigh, and her father could only agree.

'No, I'm afraid it's not,' he averred on a sombre note,
surveying her pensive features sadly. 'And I certainly
don't excuse my own behaviour, which was distinctly less
than responsible or——'

'Although at least you didn't lie about it!' she burst
out before he could finish.

'That could be a debatable point, in view of my having
kept both the affair, and your existence, a secret from
Judith,' he returned, his expression assuming an ironic
cast.

Clancy waved a rejecting hand. 'That's not the same!
You still didn't twist the facts to suit your own ends!'
Because it was that fact that caused her the most distress
and disappointment. That her own mother had purposely distorted the facts, had *used* her, as a means of
gaining some sort of revenge, she found not only hurtful
in the extreme, but demoralising too. Was that really

how her mother had always considered her? Merely as an instrument of reprisal to be used against the man who had, if not exactly scorned her, at least refused to do as she wanted? Without her realising that she gasped them aloud, her thoughts continued, 'Why, if she and Ron hadn't died when they did—leaving me free to come to Mildura, which she otherwise doubtless would have managed to prevent somehow—I could have gone through my whole life believing my father to be a cold and callous seducer who had not the slightest interest in my existence, even, let alone my welfare!'

'Yes, well, we can be thankful you discovered the falsity of that, at least,' Barrett replied, startling her, so lost in her own thoughts had she been. Then, cupping her chin in his palm, 'But no matter how governed by bitterness Estelle's thinking might have been, don't let today's disclosures warp *your* view of *her*, love,' he urged, almost as if he had read the thoughts she hadn't spoken aloud. 'I doubt she could help the way she was, any more than the rest of us can, and, when all's said and done, she did provide you with a good, stable home life.'

'If not an exactly loving one!'

'You think she didn't care for you?' He eyed her askance.

Clancy shrugged diffidently. 'I—well—ours was never a particularly affectionate family, and—and considering the way she used me to get back at you, is it so unbelievable?'

'I guess only you can answer that. But if you hadn't suspected before today that she didn't love you, then I would suggest you continue thinking the same now. And especially as I do know from the letters she wrote that she *was* very proud of you.'

Clancy sighed. Yes, she had seen that for herself when reading those same letters earlier. 'I suppose you're probably right,' she allowed resignedly, and with not a little relief.

'I'm sure I am,' her father declared reassuringly. He hesitated a moment before going on to essay carefully, 'But now that the air has been cleared, would I be expecting too much to hope you might—er—perhaps give some thought to making Wattle Grove your home now?' Without allowing her time for more than a sharp intake of breath, he continued hurriedly, persuasively, 'We've lost so many years already, and—well—' his lips quirked '—I'm not getting any younger, and we are the only family each of us has. I—I've also left you a half-share in Wattle Grove—together with Ronan—and I really would like to know that you were capable of having an active say in the running of the property once I'm gone.' His eyes sought hers hopefully, anxiously. 'And it's not—imperative that you live in Sydney, is it? I mean, even if you don't wish to sell the house, there are other options to ensure it remains in good order, and I'm perfectly willing to pay to put it in the hands of a good, reliable agent.'

Clancy bit her lip, staring at him helplessly. She hardly knew what to say. In fact, later, as she lay in bed, she had no idea just exactly what she had said. She only knew the thought of living permanently in the same house as Ronan filled her with apprehension and re-bellion—despite her being able to understand, and sym-pathise with, her father's desire.

And to her despair, thoughts of Ronan merely suc-ceeded in reminding her that he still hadn't returned to the house. Although that she should even care was utterly ridiculous, she told herself bracingly. Wasn't his absence with Lisa simply a timely reminder—if she had needed one!—of his penchant for making the most of every opportunity?

And if Lisa didn't care if she made a fool of herself over him—she was as aware as everyone else of his involvement with Madeleine—then her friend would have no one to blame but herself when she came to realise she had been nothing but a diversion for him, Clancy decided with some asperity, punching her pillow into shape with unnecessary vigour.

Nevertheless, notwithstanding her rationalisation where Lisa was concerned, it did little to solve her own dilemma and, as a result, she twisted and turned restlessly for some time before finally falling into a less than restful sleep wherein images of Ronan—the way he moved, the way he smiled, the way he kissed—appeared to torment her.

Slowly, the long, hot days of summer drifted into weeks, the weeks into a month, and still Clancy found herself no closer to reaching a decision.

She had fitted into the routine of the household without any difficulty at all. She had even assumed the role of daughter with surprising ease, notwithstanding the momentary spurt of self-consciousness that had overtaken her the first time she had spontaneously referred to her father as 'Dad' rather than 'Barrett'. Initially, the word had seemed strange on her tongue, since she had never used it before—always having called her stepfather by his first name—but now it was becoming automatic.

And she was also quite ready to admit now, at least to herself, that she would actually *like* to remain at Wattle Grove in order to spend more time with her father. As he had said, he wasn't a young man any more, and it might be their only chance to make up for all those years they had already missed. And that was quite apart from her feeling a sense of obligation to at least repay him in some small part for the Sunraysia legacy he intended bequeathing her. Evidently, Ronan had been right in that regard, after all.

But then the only thing preventing her from reaching a decision was none other than that very same man—Ronan!

No matter how she struggled to pretend otherwise, she knew she was attracted to him. Worse, she was terribly afraid she was falling in love with him as well. Resolute, self-reliant, clear-headed Clancy Munro was falling for a free and easy, fickle womaniser—the type she had been taught all her life to have nothing but contempt for!—and that could only spell disaster.

And, as if that weren't enough, her father's attempts at matchmaking were becoming even more frequent, and decidedly more obvious.

'So what do you think of Ronan?' he had probed with unconcealed interest one day while he was explaining the necessity, and workings, of the property's under-tree irrigation system. During the hot months the grove's requirement, and allocation from the river, was somewhere in the vicinity of three million gallons each week.

In response, Clancy gave a deliberately offhand shrug and allowed with feigned misunderstanding, 'He seems very capable.'

But Barrett wasn't to be diverted quite so easily. 'And on a personal level?' he persisted.

Clancy skimmed her tongue across her lips and averted her gaze. 'I haven't really given it much thought,' she evaded. 'I—I've had more important matters on my mind.'

'And it's for the same reason that you go out of your way to avoid him all the time?'

A sudden heat flooded her cheeks. 'I—I don't avoid him,' she just succeeded in pushing out faintly, discomfited at having her ploy recognised. But how else was she supposed to have protected herself against that brand of potent male allure that seemed so much a part of his manager, and which seemed to sap her will and strength with such disastrous results?

Barrett's reaction, however, was merely to fix her with an eloquent sidelong glance, and declare persuasively, 'He's a good man, you know. You couldn't——'

'Dad . . . !' The interjecting protest came on a partly despairing, partly exasperated note.

'Well, it's true. He's——'

'Ruthless, arrogant, and—and devious!' she burst out involuntarily in defence.

'Devious?' Barrett was evidently taken aback, his brows rising. 'Ronan? *Never!*' Then, with a hint of a smile, he put forward with sly subtlety, 'Although to come to such a vehement conclusion—however incorrect—one could suppose you're not quite as—umm—unaware of him as you claim.'

The flush colouring Clancy's cheeks deepened. 'Except that I didn't say I was unaware of him . . . simply that I hadn't given him much thought.' Oh, how she wished that actually was the case! Sucking in a deep breath, she took the bull by the horns. 'And if you're attempting to matchmake, I'm afraid you're just wasting your time.'

There was no denial, merely a blunt, 'Why?'

Flustered, she stammered, 'I—well—because if there's no—no attraction there, you can't force it into existence, of course.'

'You're saying you don't find him attractive?'

Would she ever forget or cease to be shocked by the instant attraction that had flared between them that very first night they met? And knowing the interested looks he received from the ranks of their female pickers alone, would her father believe her if she denied it?

'I—no, not exactly. At least, not in a purely physical sense, that is,' she qualified hastily. 'More—indifferent, I guess.' The blatant lie had her veiling her eyes with her lashes.

'I see.' Pulling at the skin beneath his chin, Barrett heaved a laborious sigh. 'Ah, well, maybe it's for the best that that's how you feel, then,' he allowed in a musing voice, and Clancy felt her muscles start to relax in relief. 'Because I thought you might like a day out, not having been anywhere else since arriving at Wattle Grove, so I've arranged for Ronan to take you with him when he visits Isla in town tomorrow.'

Clancy's stomach had lurched, every one of her muscles promptly constricting again. And, as he had begun moving past her, her father's smile had been so satisfied—so damned *knowing*—that she could have screamed. But of course she hadn't been able to either scream or object. Not then. Not without giving the lie to her claims of indifference.

All she had been able to do was stare after him in a kind of horrified frustration and hope for a miracle to extricate her. Not that one had been forthcoming—then, or in the days that followed.

As a result, she had been forced into falling back on her second line of defence. That of making her presence so slighting that Ronan would avoid her instead!

CHAPTER NINE

UNFORTUNATELY, from Clancy's standpoint, her second line of defence proved no more successful than her first, Ronan simply responding either with an irony or a seemingly mocking amusement that caused her even greater despair—he couldn't possibly have guessed the reason for her behaviour, could he?—and her father continuing to do all in his power, if with pseudo-innocence, to thrust her into the younger man's company at every opportunity.

His latest effort was to have her accompany Ronan to his cousin's engagement party that coming weekend.

'Oh, but I couldn't possibly. I mean, what about— Madeleine...?' she put forward obstructively when the suggestion was first made, both her voice and her ensuing smile deceptively sweet as she cast a sardonically brow-raised gaze in Ronan's direction.

In response, he merely flexed a broad shoulder negligently. 'As it happens, she won't be here. Her sister in Adelaide is expecting an addition to her family very shortly and Madeleine and her mother have gone down there to be with her for the happy event,' he told her in a tone as smooth as the answering smile that played about his own lips.

Clancy swallowed. 'Oh! Well—in any case, I——'

'There! You see? No problem,' Barrett cut her off, beaming his own evident satisfaction, and earning him a glowering look from his daughter even as she thought frantically.

163

'But—but I've nothing appropriate to wear. I only brought a couple of casual outfits, and clothes suitable for grape-picking, with me,' she hedged.

'There *are* shops in Mildura,' Ronan's pointed contribution came drily. 'Although it's only to be an informal party, in any event.'

'But regardless, I'm more than willing to pick up the tab for anything you might want to buy, of course,' her father couldn't wait to add, and was rewarded with another vexed and threatening look for his pains.

'That's very generous of you,' she acknowledged, albeit between somewhat clenched teeth. 'None the less, I've never even met Lucas——'

'Although you have met Isla.' It was Ronan who interrupted her this time, the barely hidden humour in his glance rattling her composure even further. 'And since she and Gus, Lucas's father, are the ones issuing the invitations...' He spread one hand meaningfully. 'In fact, she was only asking about you the other day, and enquiring when you'd be calling again. I think you made quite a hit with her.'

Clancy shifted restlessly, confused as to why he, as well as Barrett, appeared to be pressing her to attend. Merely because he was aware that her father wanted her to accompany him—including the embarrassing reason why!—and, as always, he was prepared to submit to his employer's wishes? Or was it because he knew she didn't want to accompany him—together with the even more mortifying reason for her reluctance too? Anguish billowed through her at the thought.

'As I liked her too,' she murmured faintly at last, fighting for a steady tone. Intelligent, kind and thoughtful, Isla Watkins had been so welcoming, so genuinely pleased to make her acquaintance, that Clancy had found none of the restraint usually present when talking to someone at a first meeting, and when it eventually came time to leave she felt as if she had known the older woman for a good deal longer than just a few hours.

'And since I understand your friends will also be going...' Barrett offered with a shrug, as if that settled the matter.

'My friends!' Clancy's head lifted, her eyes widening in astonishment. 'Why on earth would they be attending?' She glanced from one to the other of them, first in bafflement, and then with increasing suspicion.

'Because they've been invited, I'd say at a guess,' quipped Ronan wryly.

'Oh, very witty!' she applauded facetiously. 'Is that the best you have to offer?'

'I guess that all depends on whether there's a desire to offer more,' he shot back with just enough of an edge in his voice to have her catching her breath.

Was she starting to get under his skin, after all? All at once, she was unsure whether to be pleased or sorry. Now that it appeared she might be succeeding in her plan, all she seemed capable of remembering was the feel of his arms around her, the aching hunger he aroused in her when his mouth covered hers with such stirring intensity. Oh, damn him! she cursed silently. Why had she had to fall for a two-faced, conscienceless womaniser?

Meanwhile, sensing the sudden tension in the atmosphere, Barrett anxiously hastened to defuse the situation.

'Yes—well—it seems your two friends, Darrell and Warwick, have come to know Lucas through some of his mates whom they've struck up friendships with during the past two seasons they've worked in the district—most of the youth in Mildura know each other, if only by sight—so that's why your friends have been invited,' he explained. 'Including Lisa, naturally,' he was quick to add in encouraging accents. There was an explicit pause. 'And I'm sure she would much prefer it if you were present as well.'

Clancy grimaced inwardly. Provided Ronan was within sight, Lisa probably wouldn't even notice, much less care, if she was present or not, she reflected with acid rancour, and then promptly berated herself for such unwarranted and uncharitable thoughts. She was stupidly allowing her wayward feelings to distort her thinking, that was all.

'Or Ronan could ask Lisa to accompany him instead,' she proposed brightly as the idea abruptly occurred. Her friend would definitely prefer that even more.

'Except that I suspect Isla would rather see *you* there,' Ronan retorted on a shortening note. He made an impatient gesture. 'However, if that means nothing to you...'

Clancy pressed her lips together. 'I didn't say that!'

'Then just exactly what are you saying?'

'It's probably only a case of Clancy being reluctant to go unless she's really expected.' Barrett leapt swiftly into the breach once more.

'Unless she's expected?' Ronan's brows rose in sardonic disbelief. 'For heaven's sake, I just invited her!'

'No, you didn't!' Clancy promptly contradicted challengingly. 'Dad merely *suggested* I go with you.'

All at once, Ronan's eyes filled with amusement. 'So it's a formal request from me you're wanting, is it?' he quizzed in a lazy, faintly taunting drawl that accelerated her heartbeat.

Clancy eased the tip of her tongue over her lips, wishing she'd never given voice to those spontaneous words. 'I—well—I . . .'

'You don't sound too sure,' he mocked with a crooked tilt catching at the corner of his mouth. 'Perhaps this will be more to your liking.' His expression assumed a suspect degree of humility. 'I would be most pleased if you would do me the honour of accompanying me to Lucas's engagement party, Miss Munro.'

Disconcerted, Clancy stared at him helplessly. He was only amusing himself at her expense, she tried to tell herself, and yet still she couldn't control the maelstrom of emotions he engendered within her. No matter what he said, or how his fickle behaviour might repel her, he still had the power to overcome, with a shocking ease, whatever defences she might attempt to erect.

Now, having as good as asked for an invitation to accompany him, even if unthinkingly, what choice did she really have but to accept? she despaired. Even if she didn't do so right at the moment, doubtless her father would keep on at her until she did.

With a shaky sigh she bowed to the inevitable and finally, grudgingly, voiced her acquiescence. For better or worse, it seemed she was going to be thrust into Ronan's disturbing company once again, after all.

The party was held at the Watkins' home on the outskirts of Mildura. The acre of garden surrounding the modest, single-storey brick home provided ample space for the erection of a gaily striped marquee to cater for the smorgasbord arrangement of food and the dispensing of drinks, while the paved area surrounding the swimming-pool, complete with hired rock band and illuminating, multicoloured disco lights, lent itself to dancing.

By the time Clancy and Ronan arrived—she wearing a casual flared skirt and matching halter top in flower-splashed cotton, and he equally informally dressed in navy trousers and pearl-grey knit shirt—the rest of the partygoers were just beginning to get into their stride.

The majority of them, Clancy noted, were around her own age and outfitted in just about every style of casual clothing imaginable. They were also obviously out to enjoy themselves as the clink of bottles and glasses, voices raised in disjointed conversations and bursts of laughter, and the pounding beat of the music, all competed to give life to the proceedings.

'Which one's Lucas?' she asked Ronan as they began making their way into the throng. She hadn't yet met the man in question, and in view of both Ronan and Madeleine's comments concerning him, she had to admit she was curious.

Scanning the crowd around them, Ronan eventually indicated a blond-haired young man dancing very intimately—unlike most of the other couples—with a somewhat voluptuously built girl who looked as if she had been poured into her skin-tight trousers and low-cut top.

'That's him,' he advised, his lips twisting expressively.

'And his fiancée's name is . . . Anita?' she sought confirmation while surveying the couple.

'Uh-huh! Although that's not who he's dancing with at the moment.' His voice turned decidedly derisive, and the import of his words made Clancy's eyes widen.

'Not his fiancée! How could he possibly be showing some other female so much attention when he was only just celebrating his engagement? 'Then—then who . . . ?'

'Who *is* his fiancée—or who is he dancing with?' hazarded Ronan drily. 'Well, that's Anita over there.' He pointed out a younger girl—no more than eighteen, in Clancy's estimation—with rather winsome features and a pair of large grey eyes. 'The other one is an old girlfriend who gave him the push about a year ago.'

'Then it's a pity neither of them seems to remember that fact,' Clancy quipped, her glance condemning as it returned to the couple dancing. If Lucas couldn't even keep his mind on his fiancée now, she shuddered to think what he was going to be like later.

Anita must idolise him to be so tolerant, she surmised, and couldn't decide whether the girl deserved praise, or pity, for such blind loyalty.

Surveying Lucas more thoroughly, however, she could understand how someone of Anita's age might be impressed, notwithstanding. With his blond hair, blue eyes, and somewhat boyish features, she supposed he was quite good-looking—if one went for that type of callow, superficial looks.

Nevertheless, when she was finally introduced by Isla to her stepson and his fiancée, as well as Isla's husband, the best that Clancy could concede was that on one point she had to agree with Madeleine. Where the Watkins males were concerned, it was a case of like father, like son. They were both loud, boastful, and—overly familiar—even if, on the older man's part, it was a little less overt. Being positively leered at she had found not only repellent, but, under the circumstances, distinctly embarrassing, too.

It also made her wonder why someone like Isla would have married such a man, and she said as much to Ronan one time when they were dancing.

'I guess she's always had a soft spot for strays,' he replied on a wry note. 'Not that she's ever said as much, but I suspect she felt sorry for Gus, left with a twelve-month-old baby on his hands when his first wife died. And, since she was thirty-nine at the time, I suppose she thought it unlikely that she would ever have any children of her own.'

'I see.' She hesitated, then essayed tentatively, 'She must be disappointed, though, that Lucas didn't acquire a few of her characteristics, instead of only his father's.'

Ronan exhaled heavily. 'Yes, well, I'm afraid my arrival in the household may have had some bearing on that, unfortunately. From then on it seems, for some inexplicable reason—I don't know, resentment perhaps—to have become a case of "them" and "us", with Gus indulging Lucas's every whim and not only supporting, but as often as not, encouraging his every outrageous action.' His eyes became shadowed. 'With Isla the greatest loser, to my regret.'

'Well, at least she can be thankful you turned out differently,' Clancy offered brightly in an effort to lighten the mood, and then promptly caught her breath as a sudden, shocking thought intruded.

When it came down to it, was he altogether so different from Lucas, after all?

Where dalliance was concerned, wasn't it precisely his own free and easy behaviour that had caused her so much agonising and heartache? To date, it had already precluded her from accepting her father's invitation to make her home at Wattle Grove, for heaven's sake! So just why he should feel entitled to deride his cousin's conduct, as he had earlier, she had no idea. In that regard, at least, there wasn't much to choose between the pair of them! she decided anguishedly, the torn and smarting feelings revived by such a realisation ungovernably making her round on the cause of them.

'Or are you also looking for a female as tolerant and *understanding* as Anita apparently is?' she gibed in scornful tones.

'And just what brought that on?' Ronan eyed her askance.

Aware that she could never explain—should never even have spoken, probably—Clancy affected a deprecating shrug and contended with bitter-sweet mockery, 'A perfectly reasonable deduction. You're male, aren't you?'

'Implying, conversely, that because you're female, you're also out for all you can get?' he was swift to counter on a trenchantly cynical note.

'No! Of course all women aren't——'

'And neither are all men the same as you'd evidently like to believe!' he cut her off harshly, his eyes glinting with a steely blue spark. 'So don't make generalisations.'

Clancy angled her head higher. Then if he didn't appreciate the comparison with Lucas, perhaps he shouldn't behave in a similar manner! she heaved mutinously to herself, but forbore to say so aloud as she became aware that their unwittingly raised voices had started to draw the attention of those dancers closest to them.

Not surprisingly, though, it made the atmosphere decidedly more strained between them, so that when the band finished playing Clancy hastily took her leave on the pretext of wanting to look for Lisa. Although, as it happened, it was Lisa who found her in the end.

'Oh, hi! I was wondering if you'd be here,' that girl greeted her cheerily, taking a sip from the glass she held in her hand. 'It's a great party, isn't it?'

Clancy couldn't forestall a grimace. 'I guess so.'

'You only *guess so*?' Her friend stared at her in astonishment. 'What more do you want, especially with Ronan as your escort?' She looked about the garden expectantly. 'Where is he, by the way? Gone to get you a drink?' She took another mouthful of her own.

Clancy shook her head. 'No, he's just—' she shrugged offhandedly '—around somewhere, I suppose.'

Lisa's expression turned wry. 'And by that, do I infer that you two are—umm—at odds again?'

'You could say that,' Clancy allowed in as uncaring a tone as she could manage, and Lisa started to laugh.

'You're crazy! You know that, don't you?' she exclaimed disbelievingly. Then, with a wry grin, 'But why should I look a gift horse in the mouth? If you're not interested...' She took another swallow from her glass. 'I guess I might just try my luck with him again. You never can tell. Just because I didn't exactly light any fires in him last time...'

'No? How many hours *would* he have to stay, then, for that to happen?' Clancy couldn't help enquiring with uncontrollable sarcasm, and then flushed guiltily at her friend's look of hurt surprise.

'How should I know?' she countered defensively. 'If he stayed anywhere for hours, I sure wasn't the one who captured his attention...worse luck! He just drove the fellers and me back to the van and then left.' She made a rueful moue. 'I suspect—to see Madeleine.'

Clancy wrestled with her emotions; she was stupidly pleased on the one hand that it hadn't been Lisa to have kept Ronan that evening, and, on the other, even more stupidly despondent to learn that it had been Madeleine who had delayed him for so long.

Oh, lord, why did she have to care? Why couldn't she just be thankful she knew him for what he really was?

With a supreme effort, she injected a studiously bantering tone into her voice when at last she spoke.

'Then I'm surprised you're so anxious to try again this evening.' She drew a deep breath. 'Isn't that only playing into his hands?'

Lisa frowned. 'By attempting to take him away from Madeleine? Considering the way she behaved towards you, I would have thought you'd be the first to approve of the idea.'

'Unless, of course, he's merely playing fast and loose with both of you!' There, she had at least given her a hint as to what to expect.

But it was obviously like water off a duck's back to the other girl. 'Well, he certainly isn't with me. I haven't even managed to make it to first base yet,' came the insouciant disclaimer, punctuated by a regretful half-laugh.

Clancy sighed. 'It doesn't occur to you that, even if you did succeed in—in making it to first base, as you put it, his interest might still only be of the most—elemental kind?'

'Yes, that had occurred to me,' acceded Lisa drily, and followed with a grin and a philosophical shrug. 'But until I actually get there, I'll never know, will I? You have to be in it to win it, you know.' In the midst of sipping at her drink, she waved a hand towards the marquee. 'Oh, there's the man of the moment now! Wish me luck . . . and I'll see you later, no doubt.' With a conspiratorial wink, she hurried off in the direction of the marquee.

Unwillingly, but seemingly unable to stop herself, Clancy watched her friend's progress through the crowd, her heart jerking traitorously, painfully, at the sight of

Ronan's smiling reception of the other girl as she reached him.

Then, momentarily, his head lifted, and through a gap between the intervening people, his blue-grey gaze locked with her own. Suddenly Clancy's chest constricted and, for an instant, she felt unable to breathe, her whole body beginning to quiver at the intense look in his eyes. Then the gap closed again, breaking the contact, and in something of a panic she turned away quickly. Observing Darrell and Warwick talking to some others, she hurried to join them, needing something, anything, to distract her from the debilitating knowledge that had Ronan so much as beckoned to her, she would have gone to him.

It was for the same reason she ensured she remained out of Ronan's way for the rest of the evening; dancing, laughing, drinking, talking with numerous others, but always with the aim of making sure there was never a chance for them to be together again.

Of course, it wasn't really difficult to avoid him, she was forced to concede. She tried to tell herself that it was due to Ronan's height, at least half a head greater than most of the other men present, that she was always aware of his location among the other guests. Yet the truth was, as always, that even when she had her back to him, she could sense when he was near. Not a moment passed when she wasn't aware, acutely so, of his presence, his actions—the lithe way he moved, the deep timbre of his voice, his heart-stopping smile—*and* the fact that Lisa was doing her utmost to make certain she was his almost constant companion!

Seeing her friend clinging to his arm so possessively, flirting, inviting, aroused a rancour within her she had never before experienced, or expected to. It was churlish, wrong, she shouldn't feel that way, especially towards her best friend, she attempted to reason with herself. But it was there all the same, the jealousy. As stabbing as a hundred knives, as uncontrollable as an animal in the wild.

And it was still there when the party at last began to break up, and she had, perforce, to accompany Ronan home to Wattle Grove.

As a result, immediately they began drawing away from the Watkins' house she couldn't seem to stop herself sniping, 'I'm sorry if I'm spoiling any of your plans. No doubt you would have preferred taking someone else home.' And no guesses as to which particular one! She only wished she had thought of getting a lift herself with Darrell and Warwick.

The considering glance Ronan flicked her was unreadable in the darkness. 'Except that I always escort home the same female that I take.' His voice was coolly clipped.

'How very—frustrating for you. Perhaps you should have remembered that before insisting I accompany you in the first place!'

'Perhaps I should, at that!' She saw a muscle ripple beside his jaw, courtesy of the lights of a passing car. 'Because you've certainly got your game-playing down to a fine art, haven't you, darling?' he derided with acid sarcasm.

Clancy's control slipped a notch. Oh, lord, he hadn't guessed the true state of her feelings towards him, had he? 'I don't know what you mean,' she fenced warily.

'Not much you don't!' he disputed on an explosive note. 'But just remember, that door can swing both ways, so you want to watch you don't get caught in it yourself.' His hands tightened on the wheel. 'And the more so since you'll be living at Wattle Grove permanently.'

Clancy gasped. 'That hasn't been decided yet!' she flared, indignation supplanting the confusion caused by his initial words. Although the thought that at least he didn't appear to have guessed how deeply involved her emotions were provided some small measure of relief.

Ronan raked her with an unnerving stare. 'Hasn't it?' he countered tightly. 'You mean to tell me you can't see the improvement your presence has already made to Barrett's demeanour... and his general health?'

Clancy moistened her lips. 'Well—yes—I've noticed it.' How could she have said otherwise when she had been so pleased to note such changes herself?

'Well, then?'

Clancy shook her head. 'Stop trying to force me into a corner, Ronan! It's——'

'I'd like to do a damned sight more to you than just force you into a corner!' he broke in on her with thin savagery. 'And just might, before this night's out!' The threat sent a shiver of apprehension trickling down her spine, and she was thankful when they turned off the road and on to Wattle Grove. Soon she would be able to escape to the solace of her own room. 'Or is it just that you like to play on people's feelings?' he continued in contemptuous accents. 'Does it give you some sort of vicarious satisfaction to keep him in suspense awaiting your decision? Is that it?'

'No! Of course not!' Her voice was husky with resentment. 'While as for *you* accusing someone of playing on people's feelings...!' She gave a slightly hysterical laugh, her hand already opening the door as he brought the vehicle to a stop in front of the house. 'Well, that's got to be the greatest joke of all time!' she denounced over her shoulder as she alighted hastily and, slamming the door shut, fled up the steps.

The sound of another door closing, followed by swift footsteps, alerted Clancy to the fact that Ronan was following her—rather than having continued on to the garage, as she had expected—and she fairly flew down the hallway. She wished her father had been waiting up for them, but of course it was too late for that. After Ronan's threat, she was nervous of his intentions, and she feared she had said too much, anyway. But when she rushed into her room and hurriedly attempted to shut the door, she found Ronan pushing in behind her.

'Get out of here!' she ordered hoarsely, even as she backed away from him. His physical presence was so dominant she felt intimidated, and her breath caught in her throat as she saw him edge the door closed with his foot at the same time as he flicked the light on. 'What do you think you're——?'

'More to the point, just what was that last remark of yours supposed to mean?' he interposed to demand roughly, his eyes a glittering, turbulent blue.

Clancy's heart seemed to skid to a halt. She knew she had said too much! 'I don't even remember my last remark,' she dissembled frantically. 'So it couldn't have been important. Now will you please just leave?' She made to walk round him in order to open the door again, but by the simple expedient of leaning back against it, Ronan put paid to the idea.

'Not before I get an answer from you,' he persisted inflexibly. Abruptly he clasped her by the nape of the neck and tilted her startled face up to his. 'Now—you were saying about playing on people's feelings...?' he prompted, his gaze intent and unwavering as it held hers determinedly.

Clancy bit her lip, hating herself for being so nervous. 'I—well—Madeleine, Lisa, me—and probably heaven alone knows how many others! It makes no difference to you, does it?' she suddenly threw at him ungovernably in a choking voice.

'Doesn't it?' There was a peculiar tightness in his tone as the grip on her neck imperceptibly tightened and she was hauled closer to his rugged, masculine frame. 'Then I might remind you that it was *you* who claimed you were only interested in a little flirtation—nothing too serious!'

Colour swept into her cheeks. How could she have been so foolish and unthinking as to make such a claim? In defence, she scorned agitatedly, 'And Madeleine and Lisa? Is that what they said, too? How fortunate for you! Not to mention convenient as well, of course!'

Ronan uttered a violent expletive. 'If you must know, nothing about any of you has been either fortunate or convenient!' he rasped, and she shivered at the harshness of his expression. There was a dangerous, untamed look about him that made her feel on edge and vulnerable. 'While as for you, personally, with your *games* and your on again-off again attitude...!' Capturing her face between his hands, he lowered his head until his mouth was a bare hair's breadth away from her own and she could feel his breath, warm and unsettling, against her lips. 'Perhaps it's time for you to reap what you've sown!' His mouth closed over hers in a possessive demand that stole her breath away with the same ease as it seared through her resistance.

His tongue tantalised, pressing between her lips to taste and caress the sweet cavern beyond, and Clancy trembled, dizzy with yearning. She was nearly lost. Every fibre in her being ached for him, but at last her mind rebelled. How could she even think of allowing him to do this to her again?

'No!' she dragged her mouth from his to protest brokenly. 'If—if you must satisfy your needs... I'm sure Lisa——' His lips brushing tormentingly against hers again prevented her from finishing.

'I don't want Lisa,' he murmured.

'Th-then wait until Madeleine returns!'

'I want her even less,' he claimed against the corner of her mouth. Then, in a thickening voice, 'It's you I want. And only you.'

Clancy quivered—heaven help her, there wasn't an iota of resistance to him in her whole body!—and leant against him compliantly. She couldn't fight both her love for him and the desire he had so skilfully ignited, and for the time being she had no wish to. She wasn't made of wood. She had needs and feelings—and they were demanding fulfilment.

Now, as her defences crumbled, there were no half-measures in her response. She linked her arms tightly about his neck, her lips parting willingly to the impatient probing of his tongue. She was aware of him with every taut nerve. Aware of the hard, lean strength of his muscular body pressed so closely against her, of the caressing hands that explored the silken skin of her back, and mindlessly she strained even nearer.

With a low groan, Ronan covered her bare shoulder with his hungry mouth, his fingers adeptly releasing the fastening of her halter top so that it slipped to her waist, exposing her rounded breasts to his smouldering gaze and the searing touch of his arousing hands.

Clancy gasped, her neck arching as his lips sought the pulsing hollow at its base, and his fingers moved back and forth across her sensitive nipples. Feverish with desire, she slid her hands beneath his shirt, wanting to feel the sensuous heat of his skin against hers, wanting to touch the muscled hardness of his body as he was touching her.

Within seconds Ronan had disposed of the inhibiting garment entirely, sucking in his breath sharply when her teasing fingertips traced their way savouringly across his broad chest and curled within the light dusting of hair covering the ridged muscles. Then, almost before she was aware of it, he was divesting her of her own clothing, together with the remainder of his, and in one swift movement he had gathered her into his arms and carried her to the bed.

Holding her close, he found her lips once more in a long, drugging kiss that made Clancy turn molten inside. Sinuously she moved against him, her senses reeling at his closeness, the seductive male scent of him. Her palms coasted across the bronzed expanse of his back, revelling in the smooth firmness of his skin and, through his shuddering response, in the knowledge that she could drive him to the limits of his control, the same as he was doing to her.

Murmuring something incomprehensible, Ronan trailed his lips to her ear, slowly traced the line of her throat downwards, explored the fragile arch of her shoulder, then dipped lower still to the full curves of her breasts. Leisurely, his tongue licked at her nipples, undulated across them until they were swollen and aching with need, and she was gasping and tugging feverishly at his dark hair.

Wild sensations flashed through her, setting her body aflame. Her breasts strained closer, a clamouring hunger for the feel of more than such teasing caresses taking hold of her. Never had she experienced such a fiercely overwhelming desire, and she moaned in blatant satisfaction when at last his stirring mouth fitted itself around first one and then the other taut and throbbing nipple to begin nursing at them with an eager, tugging rhythm that sent waves of fiery pleasure pulsing through her heated body.

Now his ardent touch seemed to be everywhere; stroking over her stomach to her waist, down her hips to her quivering thighs. As he fitted one hand between them, waves of fluid fire radiated outwards to the tip of every limb, making her arch against him with a desperate urgency, her head moving helplessly from side to side.

As he sensed her feverish need, Ronan's mouth left her breasts, but only to find her lips again as he slid his hard body upward, and he groaned aloud his own pleasure at the uncontrollable sigh of satisfaction that escaped her when at last he sheathed himself within the moist, welcoming entrance to her body. His entry was smooth and deep, and, opening herself to him, Clancy responded with abandon. She lost all sense of time and place as he plunged ever deeper into her receptive warmth, her own movements matching his as she rose to meet each throbbing, breathtaking stroke.

She couldn't believe such rapture could exist. Wave upon wave of exquisite pleasure billowed through her, lifted her, higher and higher until suddenly she reached the crest ... and exploded into a spinning world of shuddering ecstasy. With a cry, she clasped Ronan to her tightly, only then realising that the spasms that were convulsing her own body were also racking his as he collapsed against her, burying his face against her throat.

It was a long time before their breathing returned to normal, but when Ronan rolled to his side and would have drawn her to him, Clancy stiffened imperceptibly. Now that cool reality was intruding once more, the sheer foolishness of her actions was beginning to make itself felt.

'I think you'd better go,' she proposed jerkily, easing into a sitting position and protectively drawing the sheet around her.

Propping himself up on one elbow, Ronan surveyed her unnervingly. 'Why?' The question was more curious than concerned.

Clancy waved a hand distractedly. 'I—well—th-there's Dad to consider.'

Catching hold of her restive hand, Ronan kissed the pads of her fingers in a disturbingly sensuous gesture. 'Although not for a few more hours yet, at least,' he murmured meaningfully in a husky tone, and she couldn't control the quiver that chased through her.

'And that's all that concerns you? Filling in a few hours?' she forced her mind back to the immediate to question with noticeable contempt. Although, if the truth were known, most of her contempt was reserved for herself.

Ronan sat up himself now, his eyes narrowing. 'No, what really concerns me is you...and your damned games of advance and retreat!' He caught her chin and forced her face round to his. 'For pity's sake, just what are you trying to do to me?' he demanded in roughened accents.

Clancy's breathing deepened. 'The shoe's on the other foot, isn't it?' she charged chokingly. 'You don't care who you hurt, so long as you get what you want! You spend all evening with Lisa, and then—and then...'

'And then...?' he prompted in a dangerously soft voice, but Clancy was too distraught to notice.

'Then you dare to use me to——'

'Not that I recall you fighting or screaming in protest!' he cut in derisively. 'It's only now that your conscience seems to be giving you some trouble!'

Clancy crimsoned. 'You bastard!' With a sob, she tried to slap his hand away, and succeeded only in so far as he captured both her wrists instead.

'Well, what did you expect me to say, for heaven's sake?' he rasped savagely, his eyes stormy as they roamed her anguished features. 'Whose fault was it that I spent the evening with your bloody vine-like friend, anyway?'

Clancy's brown eyes widened. He wasn't interested in Lisa? But before she could speak, Ronan continued in a deeper, heavier tone, 'If you remember, it was you I asked to accompany me to that damned party.'

Clancy hunched a deprecating shoulder. 'Only because Madeleine was away, and—and you always go along with whatever Dad wants,' she accused with an uncontrollable catch in her voice.

Ronan shook his head, his gaze suddenly gentling. 'Uh-uh! Not always.' Slowly he began to draw her closer. 'Just when his difficult daughter's involved.'

Suspecting him of making fun of her, Clancy pulled away, but her initial efforts to strain away from him now became a concerted attempt to free herself, albeit a futile one.

'Why?' she burst out angrily. And, wanting revenge for the hurt he had caused—was still causing, 'Because only *half* of Wattle Grove isn't enough for you?'

Ronan stiffened. 'If you were a man——'

'If I were a man, we wouldn't be having this conversation!' she interjected, incontrovertibly, on a flaring note, and after a moment's pause he gave a sudden, involuntary laugh, subsiding on to his back once more, and pulling her down on top of him.

'I should hope not,' he acknowledged drily, a ripple of laughter still in his voice as he eyed their positions expressively.

Lying half across him, her breasts pressed against his muscled chest and his encircling arms keeping her pinned there, Clancy flushed—both self-consciously, and as a result of the treacherous stab of desire that immediately shot through her at the disconcerting contact.

'Besides, aren't you forgetting Madeleine?' she gibed in defence, struggling ineffectually to rise.

A wry quirk shaped Ronan's mouth. 'Not if you can help it, apparently,' he drawled. 'Although why I should want to remember her at a time like this, I can't imagine.'

Clancy shook her head in disbelief. 'No, I can understand how it must be most inopportune for you,' she scorned, renewing her efforts to break free, although only until he moved to settle her more securely against him and the movement set her body on fire. 'You preferring "out of sight, out of mind", naturally!'

'Where Madeleine's concerned, you're not wrong,' he surprised her by openly conceding. 'Like your friend, she too has the unfortunate habit of mistaking civility for encouragement.' He paused, while Clancy was confusedly trying to assimilate what he had just said, and, sliding his fingers into her hair, inexorably edged her face down to meet his lips. 'So now, if it's all right by you, do you think we could return to the subject of Barrett's daughter?' His voice thickened slightly, and she was far from immune to the caress of his mouth as it brushed sensuously across hers.

Flustered and unable to think straight all of a sudden, Clancy could only stammer, 'B-but Madeleine...I thought...everyone said...I mean, the two of you were always together.'

'Although not by my choice, on most occasions,' Ronan contended, his lips curving obliquely. 'Hell, do you think I don't know I was supposed to be her stepping-stone to becoming mistress of Wattle Grove?' He shook his head. 'Nevertheless, the Haighs are still our neighbours, and so there are times when discussions are necessary.' His mouth assumed a rueful cast. 'There's not much I can do if she chooses to involve herself in them.'

'Not even when it's until two in the morning?' the scoffing charge was forced sceptically from her.

He slanted her a droll glance from beneath his long, thick lashes. 'I wasn't aware she had,' he claimed, and Clancy gasped incredulously.

'Then allow me to remind you! It was after you took Lisa and the boys back to the van, the night they had dinner here. Lisa said——'

'Oh? And just what did Lisa say?' One dark brow arched coolly.

'That she thought you'd gone to visit Madeleine!'

'Then once again Lisa got it wrong, didn't she?' His voice became more sardonic now. 'In exactly the same way she was wrong in believing I might be interested in becoming involved with her.'

Clancy circled her lips with her tongue. 'Th-then where did you go until that time?'

'To a mate's place, to get stinking drunk,' he told her on a harshly self-mocking note. 'I figured it might help me to forget, at least for a while, the most intoxicating and tantalising female I met in the orchard one night who was systematically turning my life upside-down!'

Clancy swallowed, hardly daring to breathe or believe. 'Y-you're not just saying that because you know it would—please Dad?'

Ronan shook his head in wry disbelief. 'My love, I may be loyal, but I can assure you I'm not *that* dutiful! I wanted you for myself. I have done since the night we first met,' he inserted somewhat ruefully, tracing a surprisingly unsteady finger along her jaw. 'And certainly not because of any of Barrett's matchmaking.'

'You really mean that?' she asked tentatively.

'What? That I didn't need your father to prompt me into wanting you? Or that I've done so since we met?'

Clancy bent her head. 'Neither,' she corrected huskily. She moistened her lips and, before her courage deserted her, blurted, 'I meant, when you said—"my love".'

'Oh, hell, yes!' A heart-stopping look came into his eyes as his fingers moved convulsively against her scalp. 'Because you are, you know. My love, and my life.' As if unable to help himself, he brought her lips down to his once more in a kiss so hungry, so scorching, that she felt as if her bones were melting. 'Lord, how much I love you! And be damned to you having to stay just for Barrett's health. It would have killed me to see you leave,' he admitted thickly, when at last they parted.

'Oh, Ronan, I love you!' Clancy responded fervently, her eyes suddenly misty with happiness. 'So much at times that it scares me.'

His arms tightened about her reassuringly. 'It shouldn't . . . because you'll have to order me to go to make me leave you.'

'Promise me?'

'Anything,' he vowed on a deepening note as he reversed their positions, and this time Clancy was the one to pull his head down to hers, with a sigh of pure satisfaction.

There were still many questions she wanted to ask, but for the moment she was more than content to let them wait. Her Sunraysia legacy was proving to be a legacy of love indeed!

This October, Harlequin offers you a second
two-in-one collection of romances

A SPECIAL
SOMETHING

THE FOREVER
INSTINCT

by the award-winning author,

Barbara Delinsky

Now, two of Barbara Delinsky's most loved books are
available together in this special edition that new and
longtime fans will want to add to their bookshelves.

Let Barbara Delinsky double your reading pleasure with
her memorable love stories, A SPECIAL SOMETHING and
THE FOREVER INSTINCT.

Available wherever Harlequin books are sold. TWO-D

Fall in love with

 Harlequin *Superromance*®

Passionate.
Love that strikes like lightning. Drama that will touch your heart.

Provocative.
As new and exciting as today's headlines.

Poignant.
Stories of men and women like you. People who affirm the values of loving, caring and commitment in today's complex world.

At 300 pages, Superromance novels will give you even more hours of enjoyment.

Look for four new titles every month.

Harlequin Superromance
"Books that will make you laugh and cry."

SUPER

HARLEQUIN

Romance®

**This October,
travel to England with
Harlequin Romance
FIRST CLASS title #3155
TRAPPED
by Margaret Mayo**

''I'm my own boss now and I intend to stay that way.''

Candra Drake loved her life of freedom on her narrow-boat
home and was determined to pursue her career as a company
secretary free from the influence of any domineering man.
Then enigmatic, arrogant Simeon Sterne breezed into her life,
forcing her to move and threatening a complete takeover of her
territory and her heart....